yeonne

Enjoy!

Hasan Richie.

# THE MEDALLION

H.P. KABIR

authorHOUSE®

*AuthorHouse™*
*1663 Liberty Drive*
*Bloomington, IN 47403*
*www.authorhouse.com*
*Phone: 1 (800) 839-8640*

*Published by AuthorHouse  08/07/2017*

*ISBN: 978-1-5462-0113-7 (sc)*
*ISBN: 978-1-5462-0111-3 (hc)*
*ISBN: 978-1-5462-0112-0 (e)*

*Library of Congress Control Number: 2017911574*

*Print information available on the last page.*

*Dedicated to:*

*My wife Rasheda, daughters Shahnaz & Tanya*
*Their husbands Tahir & Paul*
*&*
*My grandsons Zaid & Emad*

---------

*To my sister Latifa, her husband Salim*
*&*
*their children Saira, Shazia and Anwar*

# INTRODUCTION

A fiction novel based on the lives of four persons who got involved in a unique discovery found in an ancestral grave which catapulted them into the realm of extra-terrestrials living on Earth and had made it their home.

Their arrival on Earth was accidental. It all began when their world broke away from its binary system and became a rouge planet, and floated freely in space, Earth happened to be the only option to land as they sailed near about its vicinity.

Events led the four humans to be connected with the Aliens who shared a common interest in what they were looking for. Their combined efforts helped the visitors to find an object they hid in Egypt thousands of years ago. The current political situation between some nations was such that could trigger a world war, it was time the message therein in the object was vital for the survival of life on the planet.

The Aliens had all those years discretely helped mankind to progress without interfering with their beliefs and culture. They built monuments all over the then known world.

A situation arose when finally the Aliens decided to leave, it was no longer suitable to stay on Earth.

# CONTENTS

# CHAPTER 1

Sam drove up the little hill where his cousin was the parish priest of an obscure little church somewhere in England near Wales, where one branch of the family had dedicated itself to serve the Almighty, uninterrupted dedication for nearly eight centuries.

The only reason that church survived the ages was an ancestor in the 1120s acquired a little hill to serve a commitment he had made to his dying father. After his death in 1164, he was buried there by his son with an inscription on his tomb stone showing the year, his name, and words in the Middle English language of the time: 'I go with the promise to my father. Soon the truth shall prevail. I have done my duty, the rest for the world to find.'

The son had no children of his own, and fearing that there will be no one after him to carry the ancestral legend, he decided to record all he was told by his father and put it in a box along with an amulet and buried them with him. Before dying, his father had made his son promise to pass on what he had conveyed to him, and so on, until such time when someone will ask for the amulet.

Having no children to pass on what his father had instructed, before his passing in 1164 CE, he obediently fulfilled his commitment by recording all what was said to him on paper and fine leather with sketches and words, describing events that made no sense to him.

He placed the amulet between two leather skins. In a tin box, he stacked all those items and closed the lid, hammering on the sides to prevent it from opening.

After his father's burial, he waited for all to leave. Before placing the tombstone, he pushed the box as far down as possible and above it filled with gravel, tightly compacted, and placed the tombstone firmly. Having no issues to pass on the story his father narrated to him, it was safely buried for some future generation to find it.

His father had told him that they were descendants from an Egyptian priest who was powerful and who had protected a high priestess who was worshiped by the then pharaoh.

When his job was done, he sat and wondered, what that was all about, the sketches and the story of his ancestor flying to heaven sitting in a room. He dismissed the entire story as an imaginary event when his ancestor was drunk with Egyptian beer of the time. But he was contented to fulfil his dying father's wish, the family story would not be lost, or at least kept safe for a long time to come. As he walked away, he had a thought about who would find it and read the story. He laughed so loud that people stopped and looked at him. "What a crazy bunch of ancestors I have had. Whosoever finds it, will laugh even louder, unless he is as crazy as they were."

His father's two brothers were not dedicated to religious values. They also bought little hillocks not too far from the church and built their homes in the fashion of that period. They were worldlier and had little or no leanings toward heavenly commitments.

His father had told him that they were originally from ancient Egypt and that the family moved to Jerusalem after accepting the new faith. In years to come, the entire family had been overwhelmed by a European trader and adventurer who ultimately married one of the family's daughters. Shortly afterward, they moved to England. At first it was hard for them to adjust to the climate and food, but soon they settled in as one big, happy family. The family grew, and as time went by, some moved to different locations in nearby villages. With time they blended well.

After the burial, the son and his two uncles remained in close contact. There was always one in the family who took charge of the church. Most of them were buried in the churchyard. Some had names and date; others had only loving words.

The family prospered and travelled extensively, either joining the Crusades or trading. Until recently some of the family members were in close contact. Their sons and daughters inherited the ancestral properties, which were purchased in the twelfth century. Though their interests were different, they kept in touch, especially with those in charge of the church. As the years went by, less contacts led to the loss of their where about.

In present-day England, it was by accident that one family member, Sam, found a relation who was serving as a parish priest, Father Daniel. Sam was a construction contractor who had come to do a minor repair job in the church. During a break over tea, they talked about their families, and to their surprise, after exchanging their fathers' names, they discovered that their fathers were brothers. They talked at length; the priest could trace his ancestors back several centuries.

3

Father Daniel explained that the church was built by one of the ancestors and that there had always been a family member in charge until the present day. His father had two brothers; one of the brothers had died prematurely, and his son, Sam, had been brought up by his father. The other brother was a traveller and had not been heard from for several years. As time went by, he was completely out of contact with the rest of the family.

Sam explained that when he was twelve years old, he ran away from home, as his uncle, Father Daniel's father, had been very religious and had run his household in a strict disciplinary fashion. "That was too much for me. So I decided to move to a friend's house; my friend's parents were friendly and affectionate. They treated me as their own. They lived in another village, not too far from our own. His father was a construction contractor, and that is how I became one. When his son decided to get married and move away, I decided to be on my own. I was twenty-two years old and started my business." That was how Sam's existence had been lost to his cousin Father Daniel.

Father Daniel just kept nodding. "Well, that was in the past. Now we have each other, and must keep in touch; after all, we are family."

Sam and Father Daniel became closely attached. They respected each other as cousins, and more than that, they were friends.

Sam's best friend in school and college was called Michael. Their friendship so firm that Sam and Michael visited each other frequently and spent nights in each other's home. Michael was a typical government servant, with no interest in anything but his duties to his job. Sam's interest, besides his civil contractual work, was in paranormal phenomena and antiquity, which bored Michael.

Father Danial inherited his dedication to the church from his uncle, Sam's father, who had continued the work of God from his ancestors. The church exterior had been remodelled frequently throughout the centuries.

As time went on, Father Daniel had the advantage of using Sam's contractual profession to do odd jobs for the church free of cost, which Sam obediently executed, for fear of the Lord's punishment if he did not.

The graveyard housed some members of the family who had been forgotten. The few hundred or so peasants who lived in the vicinity came religiously on Sundays, stepped out to pray for the dead and on occasion performed earthly manicuring to the leaning stone slabs and collected the fallen dried leaves. That was a humane gesture from true believers.

That practice continued for centuries, and Father Daniel was no different from his predecessor or his predecessor's predecessor. He used the free services and the little charitable donations from the poor folk who were in full surrender to the Almighty.

For the words inscribed on some of the stone slabs, dust and nature took their toll, making them almost illegible. Thanks to the poor folk who performed superficial cleansing for years, which helped in keeping inscribes somewhat readable.

Day in and day out was just routine for Father Daniel. He kept the grounds as best as he could on his own, and with the occasional help from the local folk.

It never struck him to find out who those buried people were. To him they were just graves. He spent his time on preparations of sermons and how he could capture the souls of people who were about to go astray. It was a typical scenario of a dedicated person in charge of a house through which heavenly communication can be made.

Soon, all that would change, and would catapult him into a different perspective from the world he had been in, into a domain of disbelief.

# CHAPTER 2

**Ten years before,** while cleaning behind the Altar, Father Daniel was struggling with a stubborn mark below the seam at the bottom of it, using his shoulder, he involuntarily leaned hard against it only to feel a slight movement. When he realized what was happening, he applied more pressure. To his surprise, the entire Altar moved diagonally several feet. What he saw left him in a daze. He had stumbled upon a rectangular hole, exposing a narrow stairway hardly two feet wide.

His sense of adventure prompted him to rush to the door of the entrance to the church and place a sign, "Closed for repairs." That gave him an uninterrupted time to venture into what lay at the bottom of the stairway.

With a kerosene lamp, a torch, and few candles, he descended step by step into what he thought was an endless abyss. At the bottom, his poor light exposed a room. He lit candles as he ventured cautiously within. He stood at one end, and for several minutes surveyed its contents.

The room was about twenty by fifteen feet. A large table stood at one end on which were several leather scrolls, some stone artefacts, a purplish grey slate about one foot by one foot carved on it, a female figure with her hands extended upwards, on top of which a naked child sat with two little circles above the head. The circles connected by an arrow, on which a chariot drawn by winged horse. On one of the walls were some coloured sketches, below which some illegible words were engraved. "The truth shall prevail to all" which he subsequently copied and translated by a friend working in the local museum of the village. In so many days he became familiar with all the artefacts and recorded each item into a little book which he hid in his living quarters.

Once or twice a week he visited the room and spent time analysing each item. He failed to decipher any of them.

To him, it meant nothing. For months he thought of the words, but remained to have no meaning, and as the years passed by, the words vanished from his memory.

Father Daniel's dedication to the church was so, any external influence or suggestions were taboo. He had dismissed what he had found below as archaic, medieval beliefs of ignorance.

On one afternoon while strolling outside a thought struck him. "The grave yard may have some answers to what I have found down there. After all those buried there perhaps were the founders of this church and some of them go back to the 12th century." His curiosity took him running to the graveyard perched at the far end of the church.

With a bucket of water, a cloth piece he cleaned one tombstone after another. He numbered them and recorded in his private diary each and every detail. All had archaic English words, the age or dates of burial were most helpful.

"It must have been centuries that these graves lay there without knowing who they were," he thought. He realised that some may have been ancestors buried there, who had built the church.

"In there, must be the remains of my family who built the church which now I am in charge of." He pondered for minutes and as the thought sank in, he felt guilty as to not look after their resting place for years. Guilty, he tried to absolve himself from the mistakes his predecessors made by not leaving any records as who were buried in there.

The element of curiosity further enkindled a sense of adventure to find out more about the graves. But the sense of intrusion by outsiders has outweighed his interests.

It has been several years since his discovery of the room below the Altar. He kept it to himself. Exposing it to the world would intrude into his privacy and the church.

Centuries had passed since the last member of the family was buried at the church. He sorted them by the dates they were buried. The first was on January 3rd 1164, then there was a gap between 1305 and 1710. There was a gap of 405 years. The last entry on his list had no name, just a date, 1710.

Basically Father Daniel was a secretive person, the church activity must continue as is, with no external influences that might jeopardize its status.

But it was not meant to be so. It all began with a visit by his cousin Sam who had promised to do some repair jobs in the graveyard weeks ago. An easy going person a free-lance construction contractor, had no positive commitments to his clients, has decided to visit Father Daniels.

# CHAPTER 3

**Sam's pick-up truck** drove up to the little cottage near the back of the church where his cousin Father Daniel lived alone. It was about 9 in the morning. Father Daniel was nursing his little patch of vegetables and flowers which he did every morning before starting his church affairs.

"Morning Father," Sam's voice filled the tranquil morning air. His tall athletic body let his feet plough into the gravel as he approached the patch.

"What can I do for you Sam, it's a bit too early for you to visit," His voice was cold and non-friendly, without looking back at him, continued to water the plants.

Sam knew why that attitude, a non welcoming gesture. He had promised to look over the grave yard that had lain in shambles and needed a facial uplift and manicuring the little vegetation it hosted. It has been several weeks since he last promised to do the job. Sam knew that he will not receive any payment from his cousin, except that he will pray for him for doing a godly contribution to the church.

"I have come to look at the grounds and see what is needed to get the yard shining," Sam said as he came closer to Daniel.

The priest dropped the water hose, walked to the side of the cottage and turned off the water tap. He walked calmly towards Sam, "Have you had any breakfast, Come on in and join me." His invitation was pleasant to Sam's ears, "He is pleased with me," said to himself.

They sat at the kitchen table and talked in general at first; then Father Daniel put bluntly, "How long will it take to complete the work?"

"A couple of days or so," Sam voice was not convincing.

Danial knew his cousin too well to give a firm commitment, his couple of days could be couple of weeks.

"Sam, you are a good man, but there is one thing about you I don't approve of. You are quite casual in your commitments. I will give you five days, up to Saturday evening." Before Sam could say anything, Danial continued, "Hurry up with your breakfast and let go outside to survey the yard,"

Sam knew himself well that timings and dates are not his strong point. This time his cousin was serious, he gave him an ultimatum. Sam knew he was dealing with 'a man of God'; his anger would perhaps send him to hell. "Cousin, you got a deal, by Saturday you will be proud of me. Come on, let's have a look." Sam said and got up sipping the last drops of his tea.

Father Daniel and Sam were of the same age, in their mid-thirties. Sam was not a religious man in the true sense of the word. He treated life as it came. He is what you may call a free thinker. He ran a successful business in doing constructional repairs, facial uplifts to homes and landscaping. He was good at his work and his clients always came back to him for ideas and suggestions. He was everywhere and was in demand.

One of his school friends, Michael, once took him to a section of his house where he made him swear not to divulge or speak of the repair work of an underground room beneath his home.

Michael's home was on a slightly higher ground than the village, built by an ancestor in the late 12th century almost the same period as Daniel's church, just about a couple of miles away. A little stream, a burn embraced its western end.

What Sam was about to see none of Michael's relatives or friends had been to that section of his home. Being a confirmed bachelor, his secret was well guarded. They walked down to a small cellar filled with unwanted furniture, empty cartons and old paintings, all haphazardly strewn giving an unwelcoming view. Michael walked up to one end of the room where an incomplete large landscape was pinned to the wall. His finger pressed somewhere on the painting and there was a click, a door slightly opened, he held the knob and flung it open. A well of steep stairway came to view. He entered first and flipped an electric switch that flooded the entire passage with bright light.

"I did this all by myself," Michael proudly said pointing at the lights.

They walked down a few steps and entered a room. A large table with hundreds of items lay on it. Sam couldn't make anything of them. "These are collections of God knows what, were left by my father, grandfather and their ancestors," Michael said pointing to them and walked towards a passage.

Sam obediently followed and at one point there was a sharp incline and a few more steps that almost threw him off balance. They were in another room.

"We have reached the bottom. Behind this wall is a pile of rocks and mortar made by me some years ago fearing an intrusion into my home from the outside. Originally there was a door and decided to block it fearing that someone may break through. Whatever I have in here and up there can be of some value, though I haven't the slightest clue what they are worth, but I know that they are some items going back some several hundred years.

"What I want you to do is to remove this pile of rubbish and build a stone door that should look like a pile of rocks from the outside and should open from the inside." Michael said pointing to it.

The area was well lit. Sam professionally examined the crude pileup of stones through which roots of plants from the outside found their way in. "I keep cutting them, but continue to grow," Michael said and pulled at one of the roots.

Sam noticed that the paint on one of the walls had peeled off exposing a couple of bricks neatly placed. "What do we have here?" He walked up to it and using his hand rubbed away more of the old decaying paint. He rubbed harder and more paint peeled off.

"Can you see Michael, one section of the wall is made of stone, and this bit laid with bricks." Ponting to a section of the wall. "I suspect we have a door here that had been sealed and painted over. But why?"

Michael was quiet for a few minutes, thinking how to answer Sam's question.

"Sam I might as well tell you a little more about our family; it is a long story, let's go up and relax over a drink."

Sam spent a few more minutes examining and measuring the areas that needed repairs and the door to the outside.

Upstairs Sam threw himself on a large couch while Michael took a bottle of Scotch from his cabinet and poured two doubles.

"Cheers" he said and settled down near Sam. After a couple of sips,

"Just to change the subject a little bit, I have always wanted to ask you, how you know that preacher, if not being too impertinent."

"You mean Father Daniel?"

"Yes."

"He is my cousin; my father and his were brothers, and when my father died his father took charge and treated me like his own." Sam replied.

"Were you not tempted to be a preacher? It's perhaps an easy living, once or twice a week you tell the village folk what God is all about and help their souls to find the path to heaven."

"Never, the world is full of them and they are making a mess of it." Sam tone was a bit sarcastic. He got up and had a refill.

"Look Sam, now let me tell you something you and Daniel perhaps didn't know. When you mentioned that Father Daniel is your cousin that makes my father a brother to Daniel's and yours. I knew of my relationship with him but kept away, I am not fond of priests, but never guessed that you both were related.

"It's a small world, here we are finally sitting together sipping whisky. All this time we were friends not knowing your background, but when you mentioned that you are related to Daniel, I felt obliged to tell you of our parental relationship. My father died abroad, and mother soon after. I was only ten, and put in an orphanage. When I came of age my father's property and possessions were handed to me."

While Michael was doing all the talking, Sam had emptied his glass and picked the bottle and poured one for himself and Michael.

Sam raised his glass high, "Cousin Michael to your good health, I have always been a loner, and now I have you as a friend and relative."

They chatted for some time; Sam spoke of his hobbies and interests in antiquity and so on. Michael narrated his ancestral history in detail.

"How do you know all that," Sam asked

"My father kept a diary. He wrote in detail about his father and grandfather, who had kept an accurate record going back to his father and great grandfather, if I can recollect, our history goes back to the first century BCE. There was a mention, one of our ancestors, claimed to have flown in an angelic chariot far above the land. Perhaps an aging man's dream to be near God!"

What Michael had just said, made Sam straighten on the sofa, "Very fascinating," He said in a low voice, "There must have been a reason for them to record that statement, it could not have been a dream or wishful thinking, people at time had no concept of flying chariots, except in Indian mythology, and doubtful, if he had any knowledge of it. Would love to read your father's diaries someday."

15

"Who would believe such tales narrated over two millenniums," Michael murmured casually.

Sam was lost in thought while Michael was talking. His hidden interest in the supernatural and antiquities were beginning to get enkindled.

A dedicated subscriber to UFO journals and reading about abductions by Aliens increased his curiosity further, "What if they had really travelled in a space ship!"

He was now sitting with a person whose ancestor, correction their ancestor had the pleasure of travelling in a flying saucer or what are mostly known as UFOs!

Sam being a casual moody person in his profession, and had a lonely existence especially living in an obscure village miles away from the cosmopolitan city like London. His interest grew, his thoughts suddenly propelled him to the past when one day several years ago while casually walking on one of the street of London, window shopping, spotted a 'Sale' sign. What caught his eyes were the words, 'Old books, Mystery, Fiction and Records. The window display had no items, only one caught his eye, on the far end of one of the empty shelves, lay an old folding camera, of the forties. "Perhaps all other items are sold out," he thought. But decided to go in and investigate.

The shop had two sections. On the left there were people standing at the pay counter arguing with the cashier. They spoke in a foreign language. To the right, the section with the sale display card. The sign read, all items at 50% discount; books, music and miscellaneous items.

He perused around, no books or music records or discs were of his interest. He ordered for the camera and paid for it. The lady at the counter was middle aged in her early forties and pleasant. Standing on one side was a young attractive woman. Dressed in a simple dress, blue with little white flowers.

As he came to pay, the older woman just stared at him, seemed to be lost in thought, then she just said, "You seem to be a collector."

"In a way, it is a hobby, if you have anything of interest such as antiques or anything out of the extraordinary I am interested." Sam said, but he noticed that there was a certain expression on her face, as if studying him. Her eyes were transfixed on him, which made him feel uneasy. Sam's reaction was that as how to react, he however released a gentle smile filling the gap of their silence.

"You are a good man, here is my card, and if you have anything out of the ordinary, call me day or night, and on the other hand if I have anything of interest, I will surely contact you." The way she said those words were like an invitation to meet again, his thoughts were distracted when the young attractive girl extended her open palm exposing a crumbled Pound note.

Sam was already taken by her looks, but shyly avoided any eye contact or dialogue. He thought of the elderly lady, she might be her mother.

Seeing the pound note, he guessed that she might be asking for gratuity. He took out a ten Pound note and placed it in her hand. She closed her palm, "You are very generous Sir," She said.

He couldn't get rid of the lady's stare at him, "I have a strange feeling that she is either a clairvoyant or something about her that is not natural, but that young girl is a stunner."

Sam remembered his encounter at the shop many times. Somehow, it became a fixture in his mind, it lasted for months but gradually faded away from his memory.

Michael banged his glass hard on the table, "Sam I want you to be attentive to what I am going to tell you. Because of your interest in antiquity and being a cousin, I want to share with you a family secrets."

The word 'secrets' revived Sam from his reverie. Sat upright.

"Before that, let me repeat what I want you to do. To remove all that junk down there, the empty boxes and cartons, build a proper water proof door, no water or creepy insects can pass through. I was told when my mother was alive, the stream level rose and had water several feet into that room up to the passage way."

"Why not just cement block the entrance, you don't need a door there." Sam suggested.

"Yes and no," Michael said, "I have decided on the door. Who knows when I might need it?"

Sam being comical, looked at Michael, "Why do you need a door there; yes in the past century an exit like this was needed for a damsel to get in and out, visiting the master of the house, but now, the in the 21$^{st}$ century, no such precautions are needed. Unless … …" he paused and looked at Michael square in the face, "Unless you are up to something naughty, to be clean at the front door and prefer to use the good old ways. …"

"None of that. I run a clean life to keep up with family traditions, I live in an obscure little village …" He stopped and after a pause continued, "Look Sam, I didn't call you to tell me what I should or shouldn't do with my property. Just tell me, do you want to help me or not.

"Of course, all you wish will be done," Sam condescendingly said.

"Now let me tell you the family secret I referred to earlier; my mother had blocked the entrance to that room and painted the wall. Before she died, told the caretakers of the property, not to enter the rooms below as they were cursed. No one dared to visit that section, only when I came of age, and the property was handed back to me, I was told of the curse. Not believing in fairy tales, I dared to take that challenge, entered the rooms which we had just visited, but had no idea of the blocked section." Michael paused, took a sip of his drink.

Then he continued, "Sam, our family lived on this land for centuries, the roads changed, the building styles changed but luckily our property parameters remained unchanged. The passage we walked through was perhaps built when our ancestor first built the house, for whatever purpose it was used. Today, it has no meaning for me, but adds to the enigmatic nature of the residence. Here I am all alone living in a centuries old home, few people can boast of, and I want it to be so to give me the satisfaction of being different.

"As far as the bricked section of the wall, I did suspect something odd about it, but did not pursue it any further."

Sam scratched his head and looked at his cousin who was getting emotional about his ancestral habitat.

# CHAPTER 4

**Michael and Sam** spent hours going through, odd looking figurines centuries old, and romantic letters between loved ones and entries in books; one caught their attention, casually stated of a young man who had come to their home at midnight, lay at the doorsteps, and found dead by a housemaid in the morning with a small box in his hand.

On his right hand the letter Z was tattooed. He was buried and forgotten. That entry, made them concentrate on the mysterious dead visitor. They read and reread the notes several times, but found no reference to the box. The date on that page was July 26, 1817.

"What happened to the box, or its contents, there must be an explanation somewhere," Michael was now keen to solve the mystery.

"Sam, all these years I have treated this ancestral collection as items with no curious interest in going into them in details. They were there and treated them as such. Now, you found something interesting that happened nearly two centuries ago in this very house with no logical explanation to a mysterious visitor.

"He was referred to as Mr. Z, buried in the public cemetery."

Sam being a happy free-lance contractor with an adventurous attitude had nothing to lose in starting a detective's work to find who Mr. Z was. Michael accepted the challenge and both decided to dig into the village archives to find the location of Mr. Z's grave.

They thought at first it would be an easy task as all records at the newly updated Mayors building with a library fully furnished with computers and reading spaces to cater for the public and students. Records of births and deaths for the past centuries, volumes of books were now available on computers. But to their disappointment, Mr. Z was not on record.

"Impossible," Michael pushed his chair and got up, his voice sported an unacceptable looks from people around him. Humbly he sat back on his chair and looked at Sam.

Sam was thinking and placing his hand on Michael, "I have an idea, come with me," he said and both walked to the front desk.

"Can we see the books for July 1817?"

The librarian was helpful, "Please wait, and take a seat," she said and using the phone she spoke to someone.

Moments later an elderly gentleman appeared and escorted them to a room on the third floor. He climbed a wooden ladder and from the top shelf plucked a well bound red book and dropped it on an empty large table with a loud thud where Michael and Sam were sitting. "Here you are gentlemen, "From January to December 1817, all who were born and died are in there."

They flipped through pages, thoroughly examining each entry. Anything that might suggest the mysterious Mr. Z. On July 26, an entry said 'unknown,' request by Squire McKinley, is buried on July 26, 1817, family details unknown.

"Michael, your family name is McKinley, and your Mr. Z was entered in the book on the request of your ancestor. But why he does not appear in the computer records."

"Who cares, the point is that our Mr. Z did exist. Our job now to find out who the hell he was, and why he chose to die at our doorsteps."

Sam was cool and collected. He was no more that casual easy going person. He was getting into the mystery of Mr Z as much as Michael; he wanted to be more involved. It became a challenge.

"Look Michael, we now know that Mr. Z existed, we have to look for the box. It must be in your house somewhere, perhaps put away casually with some of the junk in your home. It's almost two centuries since his burial, and no one in the family bothered to find the true identity of the man."

"Perhaps those days people were less curious and soon forgotten the incident. Besides an unknown man dying outside a prominent family house best kept out from gossips, you know what I mean." Michael said casually as they left the Library.

"Sam," Michael broke the silence as they headed home, "Why not move in with me until we solve the mystery, how about it."

Sam thought for a moment, "So long as it does not interfere with my work, I accept."

What Sam had in mind was his commitment to Father Danial and perhaps find additional knowledge from the graves at the church yard.

"After all, there may be an ancestral link buried there, and we are related, we have the right to dig for the truth." Sam was justifying his involvement.

They went through the collection of artefacts but nothing found related to the little box.

An air of disappointment began to get hold of Michael, but Sam independently kept the search.

He spent many hours examining each item that might lead him to the identity of Mr. Z. To his disappointment he found nothing.

The next thing he did was to examine the wall with decaying paint. Using his tools he scraped off the paint and lo and behold he uncovered a door that was blocked by bricks and several coats of paint. "Just as I thought," he said.

Michael was not too pleased with his discovery. "My mother left instruction not to encroach into those rooms, perhaps knowing about that particular area, which is cursed. The caretakers made it absolutely clear to keep away, since, I have not even contemplated to disobey those instructions, for fear of the so called curse that may befall upon me or some innocent person."

Sam thought for a moment. He was dealing with an innocent believer of medieval tell-tale stories. He knew Michael was not the type, but perhaps being unnecessary cautious.

Sam decided to take full control, curse or no curse, "After all "I am part of the family, and have a certain right to dig into our past."

That night, while Michael was in a receptive mood, Sam put it straight to him. "Michael, you have a treasure of information down there, I promise you, without disturbing your peace, will produce to you a fascinating family history you will be proud of. Do I have your permission to go freely into the antiquated articles?"

Michael thought for a moment and nodded in the affirmative, "But avoid that room, please."

Sam was free to take full charge of the house and its hidden secrets.

What began to interest him most was the room behind the painted wall.

He almost forgot his commitments to Father Daniel; it was like a thunder bolt, forgot about the mysterious room, and thought of the church. "I don't want to anger his Lord."

# CHAPTER 5

**The next day** he assembled all what was needed such as cement, sand, gravel and a host of tools all piled up clumsily at the rare of his pick-up truck.

He thought that operation should not take more than a day or two. But he was in for a surprise.

It was Thursday morning before eight he landed at the church. He parked the pickup truck close to the grave yard and stood for a while, visually surveying the area.

He looked at the church; though he had visited the place many times in the past, he never looked at it with any depth or interest; it was an old structure with a green patch of grass in front of it dotted with centuries old tomb stones.

The early morning air and no one around, the settings appeared different to him. Father Daniel was not there to distract him.

He looked at the Church again, analytically, the grey stones it was made of stood out, the building structure archaic; "Surely centuries old," he thought.

Then he turned around and looked at the graveyard, the tombstones dotted the green patch with little or no grooming.

At one end a stone doorway made of the same grey stones the church was made of, rested near a large tree at the far corner. He walked up to it and through it. It was about six feet high and three feet wide. It was a decorative structure with no practical purpose.

From that position he stood for several long minutes digesting the scenario of Father Daniel's little world.

The centuries old church, the green patch hosting tombstones and some old trees with tentacle like braches drooping down forming a canopy.

From one vantage point he could see the village not far below, just about a mile from where he stood.

"What a sight, a scene for a painter," he thought. "Never seen it that way before, I just drive in and out to meet Daniel, I hope he realizes the beauty of the place. Perhaps an inspiration to do his good work!"

Sam examined each tombstone and chose the one near the stone doorway. The grey stone slab was reclining half of which had fallen in and needed repairs.

At first Sam using both hands tried to lift it into position. The slab was too heavy for him. He tried several times to straighten it but failed. Then suddenly the slab sank several inches down.

"The only way to retrieve it was to tie a rope and let the pickup truck do the rest," He said to himself.

Soon the stone lay flat and he stood tall above it using one foot to clear the sand. Having no success, he went to Father Daniel backyard and filled a bucket of water. After cleaning the slab he read the name and date on it. What amazed him was the date; 1164 AD., and an inscription below it that he couldn't read. It was in old English. Then he turned to the pit where the stone was resting. He put his hands as far in to clear the loose foundation of the slab; instead his hand touched a solid object other than a stone.

Using his fingers he prowled to find an object with dimensions suggesting some sort of a box or a container. He gripped it with his vicelike fingers and shook it sideways to loosen it, but the box stood firm and well rooted to the ground. He kept on for several minutes until finally it gave in. He pulled out a rusted metal box, and laid it next to him as he sat exhausted with one hand resting on it. Then, fearing Father Daniel might suddenly appear, he jumped up and ran to his vehicle, from his tool box picked up a screw driver and a can of spray to loosen the rust. Without sparing any time he was at work. The spray didn't help but using the screwdriver mercilessly pried the lid from every angle loosening the rust and crudely disfiguring the seams, he finally popped it open.

He looked in for several moments without disturbing the contents. Then he thought of Daniel that triggered a sense of urgency, and possessiveness, he gently pealed of a blank leather sheet. Then another, below which a sheet of paper, pale and almost withered, with writing and crudely drawn diagrams at one end. It made no sense to him. There were two more pages; he tried to read at random, but couldn't understand a word of what was written. Again in old English. Below the pages was another leather sheet, it was thicker. He gently peeled it off, embedded deep into another skin, a circular metallic amulet or medallion about three inches in diameter with gold and silver intricate designs. He gently inserted his right hand finger nails to free it. To his surprise the object was lighter than he thought. While he was trying to figure out the dilemma of the material it was made of, he heard Father Daniel's, "What have we here."

Sam's intention was to keep his finding a secret from Daniel, was no more, "Daniel, we have a wealth of a treasure here, can't make head or tail of what is written on these papers, and this thing is weightless," handing the medallion to him.

Father Daniel placed it on his palm and juggled with it, and bending over to Sam, "Pack up what we have here and let's go into house." Obediently Sam closed the metal box and followed Daniel who held the medallion firmly in his hand.

As they walked to the house, both minds were working on different frequencies. Daniel, greatly thrilled by the discovery and what insight it might add to the artefacts hidden below the church. His only worry was that Sam knows about the box and its contents. "He might talk to people and disturb the peace of the church. At least he does not know about the hidden treasure below the Altar or shall I tell him," Father Daniel was debating with the idea. "To allow him to share that knowledge might jeopardize the long held secrets to someone who is not dedicated to the church and expose the findings to the media and general public.

"Such knowledge may cause confusion and repercussions ..." Daniel's thoughts were interrupted by Sam catching up with him, "Father, I am dying for a cup of tea and some breakfast ..."

Daniel was working on a plan as how to get rid of Sam but, that request made him involuntarily reply, "Why not," His plans were ruined. They entered the house and Sam placed the box on the dining table, "Cousin, while you get the tea and eggs, I will spread the contents, let them get fresh air, they are very fragile after so many years, must handle them with utmost care.

"Incidentally, the date on that stone was 1164, any ideas." His voice was loud for Daniel to hear him in the kitchen.

"Not really, once we study those papers we can find out more as to who that person was." He was non-committal, he wanted Sam out of the picture. But how. His mind was working fast.

Daniel knew who that person was. After his discovery of the room below the Altar, he spent months studying whatever he found and every tombstone in the yard, dates and names. He was more versatile than his cousin Michael who had no interest in the antique treasures he had inherited from his father. The only link between Daniel and Michael is Sam, and his interest is more compelling than his two cousins from an archaeological and 'what all the mysterious' messages or records left by their ancestors or whoever that person was. He wanted to know 'what those pages say'. There were more to it than just medieval relics, "There is a message, to whom," he said to himself.

To Father Daniel, there were several gaps of missing information which now he was hopeful to fill in once the manuscripts are translated. For him that would be the end of his research. He would find his ancestral history, their contribution to build a church and the continuance of their service to the Almighty.

Sam's interest was different. "Perhaps ancestral documents left behind for future generation," He thought. His mind was working as to how he should take charge of all these findings and how they may be linked with Michael's antiquities. He did not want to involve Daniel, but wanted Daniel to be involved in deciphering what they had in front of them on the dining table.

"You seem to be lost in thought," Sam said as father Daniel stepped out of the kitchen carrying two plates. They ate in silence for a few minutes then Sam spoke in a low voice as if talking to himself.

"What do you think of all this? I wonder if there is someone who can read this stuff." Sam asked.

Daniel replied loudly with a thump of his left hand on the table. "I have a friend at the local museum who can read that stuff. But I am afraid that he might divulge the information to his seniors and we will have unwanted visitors and the media all over us. The authorities may take it all away from us and we are left high and dry."

Sam did not respond immediately. "Let's not rush into all this. We may have a solution. Let's wait a couple of days and think.

"By the way Daniel, you have been here for many years, did you find anything extraordinary at the yard or in the church premises that may have a hint on the buried people out there."

Daniel thought of the artefacts he found below the church. His face reddened, and facial expression uneasy. He was debating with himself, "If I tell him he will take away my privacy; if I don't I will be telling a lie and we will never solve anything." It took him a while when he finally said sheepishly getting up from his chair and took the empty plates to the sink, "Yes I have something, but may not be related to all this."

"Whatever it is, let's have a look, it may or may not, and why not pool in all what we have, we may find some clue to our ancestral leftovers so to speak."

Daniel was uncomfortable but was in a fix. He had to expose his hidden world lying below the church. Finally he made up his mind, "Look here Sam," his voice was firm, "Whatever I am going to tell you and show you shall remain with you, I don't want people snooping around and ruin my privacy …"

Before he could finish, Sam raised his hand, "I solemnly swear not to" in a theatrical gesture.

Daniel stood, stared at Sam not amused. "Let's go." He said and marched out of the house with a quick pace towards the church, Sam trailing behind.

# CHAPTER 6

**"I wonder what** he has that he kept to himself. Selfish, but at least is willing to share it with me" They entered the church from a back door. He bolted the door from the inside and almost ran to the church's main entrance, it was firmly bolted from the inside. He marched back and asked Sam to climb up to the Altar. Sam followed him obediently. Daniel held the Altar from one end and pushed it a few feet, the well of steps that led to the secret room below came to view.

Sam stood stunned, "The bastard ..." before he could finish his sentence, he realized he was in the church and looked up at the cross on the Altar, "Forgive me, I didn't mean it," then added to himself, "I don't want to be struck by lightning."

Daniel was already descending the narrow well with a large torch in hand, "Come on Sam, and follow me."

Obediently, Sam squeezed his large athletic body, almost sideways following Daniel. At the bottom, Daniel lit the candles that were already placed at different points in the room.

Sam stood motionless and breathless, eyes surveyed, and head turned in all directions, mentally consuming the artefacts and scenes that surrounded him. He thought of Michael's room below his house. "How similar, these items must be connected in some ways, after all the original owners were brothers and each had their stories hidden away. With time, all was forgotten." Sam thought.

He put a question to Daniel, "What do you think of all this,"

I have no idea," Daniel replied coolly. Then added, "I was afraid of bringing someone but as I said didn't want outsiders to intrude on my privacy."

"I agree, we must keep it to ourselves, after all it belongs to our ancestors and we must try to solve it ourselves." Sam was also thinking of Michael's treasures. He felt that Daniel must be involved and pool in their resources.

Sam walked up to Daniel and asked for the torch. He examined the items on the table, the scrolls and drawings. There were similarities in the sketches here and at Michael's.

He thought for a while, "Father Daniel, these artefacts go back many centuries ago, and says a lot about what our ancestors wants us to know, our families past experiences. So you must keep an open mind understanding what they want to tell us. You must keep your religious beliefs to one side, to understand what we have here."

Daniel was not at ease. "Sam, let's go up and talk about what you are telling me. Before we go any further let's try to understand as much as possible about the items in the box."

He extinguished the candles and they climbed up the stairs. At the top, the Altar was moved back in position and they returned to Daniel's home.

They sat in silence for several minutes. Both minds were working in different direction. Sam's on a scientific note and Daniel from a religious view point.

Daniel broke the silence, "Look Sam let's give it a few days, meanwhile try to finish the outside"

Sam agreed, "Daniel, any ideas as what would be our next step?'

"No ideas for the moment, get the work outside done first, then we will think of something."

Sam got up and went back to work. Then as if talking to himself, "The bastard has to cooperate," he stopped and looked to his left and right then looked up "I can use that word out here, I am not in the church."

While doing his landscaping he made notes of each tombstone and their location, especially the one which had the box.

He was tempted to dig the grave and look inside, but fearing Daniel's wrath he abandoned the idea. However, he fixed the tombstone casually in case he had the chance to dig, and find out if there were more artefacts buried with the corps.

By late afternoon, the next day, he completed what he had to do and threw himself on an empty patch and spread his legs and hands apart and looked up at the blue sky through the canopy of tree branches that spread above him.

He began to think. "Michael is no problem to handle, but Daniel is going to be difficult. His religious views are archaic, he is an ignorant fool only thinking of the afterlife, I have to convert him, and perhaps Michael can help."

He shut his eyes and let his mind wander.

He felt a kick at his foot. He opened his eyes and looked up to see Daniel standing with two mugs of coffee.

Sam jumped up athletically, "Thank you Daniel," he said taking one of the mugs.

Daniel began to walk leisurely with Sam following.

"While you were busy outside I gave a serious thought to all this mumbo jumbo affair of ours. I have no time for this, but if you want to spend your time translating all this to benefit our family, go ahead and do what you like."

Sam could not believe his ears.

Daniel continued, "Over the next week end feel free to go down there and take charge. But you must keep me informed at what you do." After a long pause, "And don't forget to straighten the Altar every time."

Sam was thrilled. He couldn't believe his ears. "The good lord is on my side" he muttered.

Both sat at the dining table and examined the antiquated pages. None could understand a single word. Daniel was frustrated and pushed the pages aside. "Can't make head or tail of all this, we'll have to find someone trustworthy otherwise the whole community will poke their noses into our affairs."

"I understand, perhaps I have someone we can trust." Sam said calmly. He thought of a person he knew in college much senior to him, nicknamed the bookworm, worked in the village library and now has an antique shop. Perhaps he can help." He thought.

"Daniel, do me a favour, get these pages copied in colour, one set for you and two for me."

Daniel meticulously picked some pages and walked to his study with Sam trailing behind him carrying the rest.

Sam put the originals and copies into the tin box and drove off. "I have to copy the medallion at Michael's he has a better copying machine."

Daniel stood outside for a while, surveyed the new fresh look at what Sam had accomplished. He was pleased. "Now let's see what he can come up with those documents, perhaps it means nothing worthwhile." He murmured to himself and walked back to his home.

# CHAPTER 7

**Michael was not** at home when Sam arrived. Without wasting time he went straight to his room and placed the box on a table, the antique treasures that lay untouched for centuries.

He poured himself a drink and stretched on the sofa. "I'll have to tell Michael all of this. He may throw some light."

Sam dozed off, to be awakened by Michael's boisterous entrance. "Dinner is served," he said holding packs of paper wrapped takeaway burgers and sandwiches. Sam rubbed his eyes and gave a big yawn. He stood up and threw himself at Michael and gave him a bear hug. Michael reaction was to push him away. "What's wrong with you, did you find a treasure.'

"Much more than that"

"Good, but first let's eat then tell me all about it."

They ate in complete silence as both devoured all what was there and sipped the last drops of beer in the bottle. Michael collected the wrappings of their meal and went to the kitchen to dispose them off.

Sam sat motionless waiting for Michael to return.

"Now tell me what the excitement is all about." Michael said dropping himself on the sofa in front of him, lifted his hands in the air, dropped them to the back of his head and stretched his legs to the maximum.

Sam pointed to the box on the table. "That box is several centuries old. Found it in one of tombs, with pages of paper saying something about that person buried in there. According to the tombstone the person buried there died in 1164 AD. The contents are in unreadable English and some sketches, like what you have down there."

Michael stared at the box. "Show me what we have here," He said jumping up from his relaxed posture.

He studied the contents, and shook his head. "This thing is beyond me, we better get some help. These things could be something, a message to tell us who we are, after all it was in a grave of perhaps of one of our ancestors. Sam, you have to find someone to decipher all this, you took the responsibility of the downstairs, now this is an added challenge."

Sam shook his head in the affirmative and said nothing. He was thinking. He had no one in mind. "The village librarian perhaps; but there is no guarantee that he will not publicize the script for personal gains. No, I have to find a way." Sam was thinking.

There were minutes of silence, no one spoke. Michael said almost in a whisper, "You have to do something soon."

Another minute of silence, then Sam sprang from his seat, "I think I have the man who can help." He thought of the man nicknamed the bookworm.

"I have a friend who I knew in college, he worked in a library and now running a small shop near about here, selling whatever antiques he can lay his hands on. Only last month I met him and fixed his shop's washroom which was leaking all over. I trust that guy. I will go to him tomorrow and see if he can help."

Next day Sam was at his shop. It was empty and no trace of his friend. Sam called and from somewhere in the store a feeble voice came from nowhere. "I am coming."

He was a man in his late thirties, but looked much older, he had some physical problems, walked with a little hunch. As he walked to Sam he adjusted his eye glasses, "Oh, it is you Sam, what can I do for you."

"Look Jim I need your help." Sam came to the point.

"How good are you at reading some old manuscripts? Very old ones. In old English, to be exact Middle English. We are talking of around the late twelfth century."

Jim looked at him, scratched his head and stared hard at Sam quizzically.

"Sam that should not be difficult. Come next week, I am busy with some arrivals and …"

Sam cut him off.

"Look Jim don't give that tune, I want you to start right away. Yes, right now. Close your shop and let's start. I will pay you well."

Jim looked at him and smiled. "Sam I never found you a person in such a hurry. It took you two months to come and fix my toilets. Just be calm and take a seat."

Sam sat in front of him across the desk and placed the copies of the documents. Jim picked one page, looked at it for a minute, then without looking at the rest he pushed them aside.

"Look Sam, translating these pages will not be easy. It is a dead language we are dealing with. Beside me, I have to go to an expert who knows the history of the time. These pages as you say perhaps go back hundreds of years ago. I have a retired friend who worked in the city's museum for more than twenty five years."

Sam did not like the idea that an unknown person is involved, and can he be trusted? He may pass it on to someone for financial benefit. Sam was uncomfortable. He was not sure what to say, but had to make a decision.

"Look here Jim, this is a family matter, and I don't want others to be involved."

"Sam, if these pages are genuine, they are a national treasure as far as I can tell from my first glance, and then, God knows what will become of them. Think carefully now, you want to go ahead or not.

Sam was silent. Thinking. "If I agree, I have one condition."

Jim was listening.

I want to go with you to your friend and have access to sit with him while translating."

"Sorry Sam it does not work that way. The man is retired, and may work on the papers at his own leisure at home. Of course, I will be with him sometimes to assist if need be. I'll ask him if you can be with us. What I will do to arrange for both of us to meet him and see what he says."

Again Sam was not sure as to what to say. Then he thought of the room below Michael's house and the one below the Altar in the church. Sooner or later he has to tell Jim, and his friend the retired museum man, may be involved. How will Daniel and Michael react?

Sam had to make a decision fast.

Sam looked squarely at his face. "Look Jim, I have no problem with you, I trust you hundred percent, but to be honest I don't know your friend. What I suggest is that we sign a confidentiality agreement just as a formality. You see there is more to tell you besides these papers. Perhaps your friend will be more involved."

"Sam you are making this issue more mysterious than meets the eye. I am beginning to sense an element of some sort of historic finding you have stumbled on. Why not tell me ..."

Sam interrupted, "In due course, when we have deciphered these pages. I promise to tell you everything. As far as I am concerned you will be the main figure to conduct this operation."

Jim shook his head in the affirmative, "Ok Sam let's get started. You can take your papers and come tomorrow morning with them, and go to meet my friend. His name is David, so until then." Jim got up and accompanied Sam to the door.

Jim went back to desk and sat down stretched his feet and leaning back. "What am I getting into, a disaster or fame?" he said to himself.

# CHAPTER 8

**The next day** Sam was at the shop at 9 in the morning. He placed his brief case on his desk and took out a page and placed in front of Jim.

"What is this," Jim asked

"The confidentiality agreement to be signed by you and a similar one by your friend David.

Jim read it and signed it.

Minutes later they left the shop to meet David. Jim had already spoken to him and agreed to meet at a restaurant to have breakfast. .

When they arrived, David was already there having coffee. He stood up to meet them. David was taller than them and shook their hands firmly. His face had a permanent smile and sported a short daggered salt and pepper beard. For his age he looked ten years younger. Sam liked him at the instant they met. They socialised for several minutes. Apparently Jim and David go back to several years of friendship. Sam sat and nursed his coffee allowing the two to have their fill of old times.

During breakfast, the subject of Sam's documents came up. David talked about people who had relics that go back to the fourth and fifth century. "But what Jim told me about your findings interest me, I can help you, it is like a hobby to me. We can meet at my home and work together, I have all the time, I am retired and we can work at leisure."

Sam could not have heard better word from David. He was open and straight forward. He was friendly and approachable. Sam felt a bit embarrassed to ask David to sign the confidentiality agreement.

To his surprise, Jim brought in the issue to which David accepted gladly.

"This is business, why not."

Jim spread the page and David signed.

It was agreed to meet at David's home the next day. "Sam bring in what you have, so until tomorrow, all the best." Sam and Jim shook hands with David and left.

"Jim, I like that man. He looks the type I can trust. Inviting us to his home from our first meeting shows his simplicity and genuine interest in our venture."

Jim did not say anything, but told Sam to come to his home at 9 in the morning the next day and drive to David's home. "He lives not too far from us, just about thirty minutes."

The next day, they arrived at David's home. He met them cordially and took them to his study. There was a large desk surrounded by shelves stacked with books and folders. Two chairs in front of his desk with a little table between them. On the desk, there were two lamps, a small one and the other with higher stand, flooded the top of his desk. The curtains were drawn.

"Come in gentlemen into my little world. I am alone, no wife to make tea, but if we are lucky the maid may bring in some."

Jim whispered to Sam that his wife had passed away several years before. His two sons live in London, but come to see him on weekends.

"David, here are the documents I talked to you about," Jim said spreading them on the desk. He placed them such that the light from the top displayed them clearly.

David walked to the other side of the table and put his reading glasses bent forward. For several minutes he studied one page. He said nothing.

Jim and Sam just stood across the table looking at David's bent posture trying to read.

Minutes later David straightened himself. He removed his reading glasses. He looked squarely at Sam. "Of course these are copies. Do you have the originals?"

"Yes."

David did not give Sam time to say more. David sat down on his chair and requested them to do the same.

"Sam, what we have here is a kind of history book. I have managed to read a few lines and it looks that the person who wrote this, was narrating what his father had told him about his ancestors."

Sam just looked at David saying nothing. Jim made a facial expression of appreciation.

David was brief, "Gentlemen, leave this with me for a couple days and let's meet say in about three or four days. "Jim, I will call you to fix a date." He looked at Sam, "Don't you worry, and the papers are safe and sound with me."

Sam was relaxed, he trusted David. Getting up from his chair he extended his hand to David in a warm handshake. "Thank you David." He said heartedly.

Sam briefed Michael of his meetings with David. He assured him that he was with the right man to help them decipher the documents.

Michael, after the brief adventure of not finding who the mysterious guest known as Z, lost interest in getting more involved, but he had left it to Sam to continue, "Sam, I have authorised you to handle all this mysterious discoveries, and when you have solved it, let me know. For the moment, I want one thing from you, complete the work downstairs as soon as possible."

"Michael you are a great guy, I will not fail you." Sam was more patronizing and meant what he said.

David had said that he will contact them in three or four days. Sam took the opportunity to start work at Michael's home.

He began immediately. He sat on a stool and studied the room, looked at the relics and sketches, then at the door to the outside.

He looked at the wall where he previously brushed off some of the decaying paint. With a spatula lifted more paint, became more curious, and began to scrape off the paint covering the bricked door.

"I must get to bottom of this, curse or no curse, I am getting inside. Come what may," Sam said to himself.

When done, he removed a few bricks that came off easily, sufficient to peep through. With a torch, he surveyed, allowing the light to move from one side of the room to the other. Could not see clearly, widened the orifice, and let his torch light to scan, a chair, on it, in a sitting position, was a human form. He was horrified, but dismissed that uncanny fear, and continued to let his torch to survey minutely the contents of that room. He found a raised section, like a tomb with a slab of stone on it. The mystery of that room had more to say than just a branded curse. "Someone is buried there, but who? And why all the fuss?" Sam was intrigued.

That set fuel to the fire of his probing, he dislodged several more bricks and decided to enter. Still the element of dread haunted him, he stepped in cautiously. He stood for long minutes and examined the room from side to side. It was small. A room turned into a burial place. On the tomb, some crudely etched writing. He envisaged to be the burial of a person with very little decorative ado, to be tucked away, and forgotten. The human form on the chair was an empty suit, close in resemblance to present day contamination suits worn in infected locations. On the left sleeve were some kind of nipples with inlets, the material, close to thick synthetic rubber.

"Who wore that suit?" He muttered to himself. "No one at that time could have had such an attire," he paused to think, "Unless he was connected with some scientific research or perhaps he was a space traveller. A wacky idea, and as weird as the ancestor who travelled in a chariot in space." He nestled next to the chair, and was lost in thought.

"The person buried in here must be connected to the family, perhaps a space traveller or involved with that kind of stuff. Poor Michael, does not have a clue that in his own house a space traveller ancestor is buried right under his feet, crazy at what it seems.

"But how is he related, and be buried in the house?" Those questions created more puzzles to the mysteries they had at hand.

"Michael, Denial and I are related through our parents, now with the recent finds we have a direct link to our past ancestors who were somehow connected or involved in some kind of past extraordinary events." He then thought of David, and Jim. "May be they will come up with some explanation after deciphering those enigmatic pages." With those thoughts Sam decided to go up and relax, wait for Michael and tell him of his findings.

Michael was already back at home, reading a newspaper and enjoying a drink, "I came back from office and decided not to disturb you, how is the work down there?"

"As good as it can get." Sam replied, but had to tell him of his entry into the cursed room, finally he spilled the beans, "Michael, I want to confess, I have disobeyed your instruction, and I have taken the liberty to enter the cursed room."

"What!" he exclaimed. Then after a few moments, he curiously asked, "What did you find in there?"

Sam was relaxed, he narrated his findings and what he thought of them.

"I had warned you, not to let your curiosity get the better of you, but you have dared to take up the challenge, you found a secret that lay within, perhaps the family then created a parable to prevent anyone to probe into it. Had it not been for your daring plunge, the mystery of that room would have remained unsettled.

"Sam, I agree with you, until we decipher what is on those pages, we should hold on from further activity. Only then, pool in all our findings, and come out with a brighter picture. As far as the person buried down there I haven't a clue. My mother just instructed, that the room was cursed and nobody should try to enter it.

"It is obvious, a relative, he or she was buried down there, must be for a reason. Let's wait and see, perhaps we come out with an answer."

Sam nodded with a quite yes and quaffed what was left in the glass and went for another fill.

Early next morning Sam got a call from Jim.

"Jim it better be good to wake me up at this unearthly hour."

The exited voice of Jim rang hard in his ears. "Sam, you better come over to David within the hour. I will be there. Be prepared to learn where you come from. Bye for now."

Sam showered, had a quick breakfast, jumped into his car and away he went.

He let Michael enjoy his sleep. He just left him a note saying "Had to go on urgent business."

Jim was already at David's when Sam arrived.

After exchanging a few polite niceties David asked Sam to sit right in front of him across the table. Jim sat next to him. On the table were the pages Sam had given David to translate. All were placed next to each other, brilliantly lit by the top lights above his desk.

Having all settled down, David looked at Sam "What we have here is an incredible bits of history. As you have the originals, no one can challenge or dispute the authenticity of what we have here."

David paused for a few seconds and added, "There is a mention of an amulet or medallion that was given to your ancestor to keep safe until it will be needed by those who gave it to him. I am at a loss in the sense that those who gave it to your ancestor are not alive now, unless …" David stopped, "Of course would be their descendants who will ask for it. Too difficult to suggest anything right now. But for the time being what those pages say is simple, though at the end there is an element of science fiction stuff such as in today's language refers to extra-terrestrial visitations. Anyhow, we'll come to that when we go further more through the pages."

Sam was in a dilemma as to what to expect. However, his interest in the supernatural and UFOs were more of an interest to him. He recomposed himself into the chair and leaned forward across the table, as not to miss a word of what David was about to narrate.

"I have made a translation which you can read at leisure. Meanwhile, let me narrate what those pages say,"

David began, "My name is Richard son of Simon I have no children of my own to pass on my father's story, which he got from his father who had told him what I am writing here. According to my father, the story had come down the line from father to son going back many years before the birth of the Great One." David stopped and interpreted the Great One as meaning Jesus and continued to read. "Our ancestor worked in an Egyptian temple in

Egypt, as a priest in charge to look after the upkeep of the temple. He was respected by all including the Pharaoh. In that temple, a High Priestess resided, and was worshiped as a goddess, she had some powers to heal the sick and predict good and bad future events. All were afraid of her.

"To fulfil my father's wishes, I am putting all what he said and the circular amulet in this box, for someone or a relative, to ask for it."

David stopped reading, and looked up to his stunned audience. "There is no further mention of the amulet, whatever it is; it is for us to find out. Let's me continue, coming back to the story, so he leaves all that he has written in a safe metal box for someone to find, and read the story of his father and ancestors."

"What about the rest of the story, it's not finished? The UFO bit etc." Sam voice was demanding.

"Easy my friend, I have yet to come to that, just sit and listen." David spoke in a low voice.

David adjusted his glasses and began translating, "Oh yes, here we are, the paper continues with their ancestor being caught sneaking around at some mysterious bright light near about his home. Out of the light two persons walk up to a house near him and seconds later accompanied by two female which he recognised as his neighbour's daughters.

"Hours later he saw the same bright lights with the daughters accompanied by two persons. Our ancestor thought that those men were demons and he decided to keep away.

"This mysterious bright light comes and goes at night with young men and women going in and out of it. One night the ancestor was caught watching them. Before getting back into the bright light, one of the escorts stopped and walked up to him. He extended his hand and asked him to go along with him. Frightened and nervous he obeyed.

"Crossing the bright light he found himself in a room. The room was not made of mud bricks, it was spacious and the lights were dim but there was no source of lamps, light was just there. A person walked up to him, he was human in looks, a little taller and had a pleasant facial expression. He was told that he was chosen to help them and not to be afraid.

"Few days later the ancestor was elevated by the Pharaoh to the rank of high priest with more powers to look after the Temple and the priestess. The same night he was visited by the mysterious man who took him into the bright light and the dimly lit room.

"He was introduced to a second person who explained to him that they were not demons as he thought, but people like him, come from another world. He did not understand what they meant, then felt a sudden movement in the room and he was told to look out of a window. The ground receding away, then he thought he saw the moon, but was told it was his world, many many cubits up in the sky. To make it simple for him, he was made to look through a window and see the ground come closer until could recognise his surroundings. He felt blessed to be taken up to heaven by a flying chariot with all the comforts of a room.

"They explained to him that the men and women they took were given some powers to do well, and the women will bear children who will benefit the masses. The ancestor could not understand what they told him, nor did the writer of this anecdote."

David put his reading glasses down. "Gentlemen, what we have here so far, says a lot. The final line just says, that some years later one of the great grandsons of the priest moved to the Holy Land, and years later with the help of a man from a northern country married his daughter, took the whole family to his land where they settled and made it their home, and built a holy house."

David took off his reading glasses and put them on one of the sheets. No one spoke for a while. Sam looked at Jim and Jim looked at David for some answers.

"Incredible story, no one will believe it. But as David said as long as we have the originals we have a great story," Sam put in.

David interrupted, "Look here Sam, it is not easy, unless we find out what that medallion is all about. Secondly, do we have any kind of family book or artefacts or whatsoever, that came down the line from an ancestor who moved over to England from the Holy land and built a church and a home? What was the year and how are we going to trace that family through the centuries, no doubt, some more may be buried along with persons or in other locations. It is not an easy task. Only when we find the links and some more information, we can go ahead."

Those word sent Sam's mind working, he may have some of the answers that David was referring to. "Shall I tell them?" He thought for a while and got up from his seat.

"Gentlemen, we do have a mega story here. I have been a UFO freak since childhood and the last bit on those pages make me believe that it was my ancestor who *met and worked with extra-terrestrials and travelled in a spaceship.*" David and Jim just listened.

"It must be our family we are talking about here. We are three cousins, one is a government servant, the second is a priest and myself. I must confess that I do have some more information that may perhaps help us solve our search for the truth. As far as the medallion, it is with me and I have no answer what it signifies.

"At my cousin's home we have a treasure of artefacts and at the parish church where my cousin Daniel is the parish priest; there is more to add to this enigma."

Sam was not worried about Michael's cooperation. Daniel may be a problem.

When Sam narrated what he had achieved with David and Jim, to Father Daniel, there was a reaction to the contrary from what Sam expected, "Sam I can't believe it, it sounds like fiction to me. So, come to think of it, our ancestor was perhaps the first person in space." After a pause he said with a comical facial expression, "Not Yuri!"

"Bravo, well said Father, our family will go down in history once the documents and artefacts are proven to be authentic, to achieve that goal, David and Jim would surely spare no time in accomplishing that task." Sam said assuredly.

"How long he will take to complete the study?" Daniel voice more eager.

Now he has Daniel approval to get David and Jim to work on the church, and Michael's antiquities treasure trough, Sam had no problem in getting in and out in both places, to conduct their research.

# CHAPTER 9

One night while lying in bed thinking about the stories from the pages left behind centuries ago, especially the extra-terrestrial bit, Sam thought and thought and thought, he came to the conclusion of them being authentic, "People at that time had no way of thinking of extra ordinary *beings* of visiting and talking to humans and to top it all, converse about *Space*.' He jumped out of bed and sat with his hands cupped on his head. Then he remembered the lady and the beautiful young girl at shop where he bought an old folding camera. He remembered the words of the lady, "She said something like, if you have anything out of the way come to me, I may be able to help."

He got up and went straight to his brief case. "Her card should be here somewhere.' He murmured.

It has been some years ago, "Her visiting card must be somewhere in the brief case I have no other place to store my official papers." After going through item by item, he finally found it clipped to a page inside a folder.

He read her name loudly, "Ayond Flagstone, What an unusual name, I hope she remembers me and can help us."

The first thing in the morning before breakfast he called her number, on the first ring a soft female voice answered, "Good morning, the director's office here, what can I do for you?"

"My name is Sam, and I want to speak with Ms Ayond ..." suddenly there was a click and another voice spoke. "This is Ayond here, what can I do for you Sam?"

"How did you recognize me and my name so instantly," Sam was happy.

"Very simple, as soon as you mentioned your name, our computer picked you up from our file. You have been recorded as 'Sam who bought a Camera'. I was interested in you the moment we met in my shop. I had a feeling that someday you will have something interesting for me. You were on my special list. That's why the moment you mentioned your name, the computer picked you up. You have something interesting for me that you called?"

"I have plenty to tell you, but I am not sure if you are interested in fairy tales about Space."

"Try me," was her instant reply.

They agreed to meet the next day at a coffee shop not far away where Sam lived. Her address on the card showed an obscure village not shown on the map.

The next day Sam arrived at the coffee shop. They talked in general and Ayond began, "We have been living there for many years, in fact we were the first to buy land in that area. It was an empty plot far from any habitation at the time. Even now there are just a few houses, far away from the madding crowd as they say." She said with a smile as she sipped her coffee.

"Look here Sam, let's not stand to formalities, and let's speak our minds freely. Now tell me what you have."

Sam explained his relationship to his cousins, Daniel and Michael and the antique findings at their premises. Copies of all the pages found in the box, and the medallion were put in front of Ayond.

"I brought these, may be you can help me to understand them better. Perhaps not of your interest," Sam said pointing at the papers and medallion.

"Sam," she said softly and waited awhile, "I don't believe what is in front of me. Now, once again, tell me from the beginning how you came about all this. The medallion specially. How many people know of all this?"

He narrated in detail the whole story, and the contribution David and Jim made,

"Do you trust them?"

"Michael and Daniel are my cousins, the artefacts and all these were found in their premises, as far as Jim and David are friends who translated these papers. I fully trust them."

"You have invited me to help you, in which way?" There was a long pause, he guessed the interest in her tone.

"You trust me, otherwise you would not have shown me all this. I accept to help you on one condition. No one else shall be involved, relatives or the gentlemen helping you," she said firmly.

"But that is impossible. They already know so much, it be difficult to disassociate them now."

She raised a hand "I understand your position, in that case, I have a proposition. Let's have a meeting with the two gentlemen who are helping you, and a separate meeting with your cousins. I have a way to make my own judgement."

"That's great, I shall arrange the meeting whenever convenient."

"Tomorrow any time, we can have two meetings, one in the morning and the other in the afternoon," Ayond suggested.

Then Sam put in bluntly, "You seem to be thrilled to be associated with all this. Is there a special reason, perhaps monetary gain?"

Before he could finish, she interrupted, "I want you to put it out of your mind that there is no monetary interest, and let me tell you, what we have here can affect the whole world. You have stumbled on an issue we have been waiting for. You have no idea of the task before us. In the wrong hands there can be life and death."

Sam just stared at her as she spoke. She was not the soft person he knew. She was now in command, has become the boss without Sam realising it. She was business like.

After she left, he sat at the table thinking. "She said it will affect the whole world and it is a matter of life and death, what did she mean, who is she to utter those words, unless she is a part of an organization," he kept analysing her words. "What am I getting into?"

At Michael's home, Sam spent the evening alone. He was contemplating his next move to arrange the two meetings. He rang

Jim and David to meet the next morning at David's home. He told them that the meeting is urgent as it involves more information. They agreed.

When he spoke with Michael, he excused himself, he just told Sam, "Do not bother me, I have given you full authority to handle the situation, I can meet this friend of yours some other time and have tea with him."

"It is not him but her," Sam corrected him.

"Whoever and whenever ..." Michael said then changing the subject, "I have to leave town on an official business tomorrow, and will be back in a couple weeks."

Next was Father Daniel, he decided to meet him rather than on the phone.

He arrived at Father Daniel home early morning before going to the meeting with Jim and David.

To his surprise he found him to be more receptive and understanding. Sam's careful deliberation which sounded more or less like pleading so as not offend him in any way, went on and on ...

With a wave of his hand Father Daniel interrupted him and said softly, "You mean to say that these people can translate and read what those drawings mean. As long as the church's privacy is observed and can't have people running in and out during official church hours I have no objection. You must sign a confidentiality agreement to shut their mouth to put it crudely."

Sam could hardly believe his ears. "Father Daniel sounded keener than expected. After all, the element of curiosity exists even with in some of the strict religious fanatics." With those thoughts he quickly excused himself and headed for his meeting with Ayond, Jim and David.

They met at David's house. Chairs were arranged around the desk with one set of copies of all the documents in front of each.

Ayond sat in the centre. Introduced herself and picked the sheets one by one. There was pin drop silence as three looked on, waited for her to speak.

But it was David who took the initiative. He cleared his throat, and gently looked at Ayond, removed his reading glasses. "Ayond, that is an unusual name, it is very nice sounding as if not from this world."

Jim laughed and added, "It must be French."

Sam was quiet.

David interrupted and said politely "Didn't mean to be disrespectful, just my way to be friendly."

"I enjoyed it, especially the bit 'not from this world'," she put in coolly.

"Why is that," Jim asked

"Because I am not from this Earth," Ayond said tunefully.

"You are too beautiful to be an alien," Sam put in.

"Have you seen what an alien looks like," Ayond turned to Sam.

"Not in real life, only in Hollywood movies."

"Forget what Hollywood say, it is all rubbish," she said calmly.

"Well, whatever you are, French, Swedish or Indian, all ok by me, I like your sense of humour," David put it with a smile.

"Any way let's start with what we come to do. Who has that medallion?" Ayond asked changing the subject.

Sam handed it to her.

She looked at it on both sides. "The obverse has a function and the reverse has a function. The medallion is a key to something, it has been misplaced or rather forgotten as who kept it."

"How do you know all this? Is it written anywhere?" David asked

"I just know. Because I have been waiting for it to show up."

The remark by Ayond left the three dumb and speechless. To Sam it was probably her manner of saying 'we know about it', a form of sarcastic humour.

To David and Jim it sounded like she knew what the medallion was, and knew more of what they talked about. She was perhaps a government agent.

Jim asked bluntly, "You seem to know more than what is written in the scrolls, are you working for a government agency, why don't you come out openly so that we know whom we are dealing with."

Sam was embarrassed with Jim's blunt attitude. He was attacking Ayond's integrity, after all she came because of him.

"Look here Jim, you are not being civil accusing ..." before Sam could finish, Ayond interrupted.

"Never mind what Jim had said, it was because the way I said it. In fact it is true what I meant. I should have introduced myself fully when we met. Even Sam does not know, let me introduce myself properly. You gentlemen are respectable citizens; David you are a researcher and retired, a kind of scientist, Jim you are in the antique business and I know how secretive when it comes to your professional ethics, and as far as Sam is concerned he is a man I can trust blindly.

"I was coming to that after the meeting. But let me tell who am I, what is my interest in this project and how you all will benefit from it, not monetarily. That will be known to you in due course."

She paused for a long moment, studying the faces of the three. "As I said earlier I am not from Earth that is a fact, jokes aside. "And," looking at Sam, "We are a beautiful race as a whole. You all should come with me and look for your selves. Perhaps after we finish what we are doing we will make a trip."

"Ayond, unbelievable, you mean to say that we are actually sitting with an extra-terrestrial, an alien," Sam said quizzically.

"Yes Sam it is so. We have to know each other more intimately."

David and Jim were silent, gazed at Ayond.

Jim was first to speak, "Please forgive me for say those things earlier, I meant no disrespect," after a pause he added, "We earth people sometime speak out of turn without knowing the facts."

"Nothing to worry, we too have similar situations," Ayond said, looked at Jim and placed her hand on his.

David was quiet, not knowing what to say. Then drawing every ones attention, he gave a gentle cough followed by "Oh, I must add that the whole atmosphere in this room has turned enigmatic, we are actually talking to an alien from another planet, sitting together trying to solve an earthly problem?"

No one said anything. Another few moments of silence then David continued philosophically, "All is well and good to have 'an alien' among us. Because of her goodness to be one of us in our hour of need to solve an ancient message which may have an effect on the human race. What will be the role of the aliens and ours in all this? How the world will respond, there might be repercussions."

Ayond was prompt to reply David.

"David do not be a pessimist, it is too early for that. We have a mission to accomplish first, and then we can tackle the inevitable."

"Agreed," David murmured submissively.

"Now shall we get on what we have come for," Sam muttered. Then he requested Ayond to speak. "You seem to be more versatile than us in all this and what is scribbled on these parchments, so please tell us what it all means."

"I will tell you exactly what the inscriptions mean. Please do not interrupt, when I finish you can put any questions." They all nodded.

"Ok gentlemen here we go.

"A gentleman of responsible attribute was in charge of an important temple in Egypt, and the protector of a high priestess who also lived in there, was worshiped by the then Pharaoh. The priest witnessed a spaceship taking girls and bringing them back. He was caught by the spacemen and was taken into a spaceship for a ride.

"He was treated well and they liked him. Their contacts remained for a long time, and taught him many interesting applications to treat sickness and insight into things to come. He was entrusted with this medallion, which is with you today, to keep safe and pass it on to his son before his demise, to keep, and pass it on until someone will ask for it. As far as the sketches, it is not clear what the little boy or girl on the sketch mean, I will check in our archives and let you know." Ayond stopped then looked around, she said, "Oh, I smell tea. Let us first enjoy a good cup of hot tea."

Just then they were interrupted by the entrance of a housemaid carrying a tray with a tea pot and cups. She served them and left.

"Very interesting," Jim was appreciative.

"Talking about the little child I had another notion, I thought the child in the sketch represented someone from another world to benefit the human race. As I said the sketch is not clear, the wings may mean a travel, the two circles above their head does not mean anything to me unless," Ayond paused and thought for moment, "Unless it indicates power,"

David interrupted by putting in, "Or some kind of an indication that he or she was special or 'holy.'"

"We don't know, let me search in our files. We may have some indication in the church or at your cousin Michael collections.

"The medallion is going to be difficult. From our records a 'key' was kept with the priest and to be passed on to his son, and his son's son until the time when someone will come and ask for it. That someone will know who has that key or the medallion, where to find it and *where to use it*. All that should be written in our records. The only thing I know, is to search for the medallion, as ordered by our boss. We have been looking for it."

"As we have it, you can do some digging to find out more, or perhaps your boss can help." Sam put in.

"The medallion was handed over to the priest much before my time. I came into the scene just about two centuries ago. However, I will check our special vaults which has not been opened for many years. It probably has a lot of information better kept away from humans, they are not ready for it."

"Why not, we are civilized enough to take anything," David said with confidence.

"You may be and a few others. But a lot in this world are not. Perhaps another 500 years," Ayond corrected him.

"Well hard luck for them, why should we be deprived. Let everyone know the truth even if it means social upheaval. In due course it will settle down." David was blunt.

"That is not very nice thing to say David. Let's leave it at that."

"I don't know why we the civilised part of the world have to suffer just because there are dumb and illiterate people who have chosen to be so for the sake of their medieval beliefs and so on, I can go on, don't you see what I mean," Jim added.

To change the subject, Sam interjected, "Perhaps sometime in the future when Ayond is more relaxed and gets to know us better, may invite us to her library and show us a few things of interest."

David asked, "Madame Ayond, you just mentioned that you came to the scene some two centuries ago, that makes you more than two hundred years old."

"Don't let my age bother you, by our time scale, I am just about fifty, and as far as visiting us, I will arrange it."

"Now where was I," Ayond said, gathered her thoughts. "O yes, the child with the two circles above his or her head. It could mean 'to rule' as in ancients sometimes used a circle to indicate handing over authority. These are all speculations."

"So Ayond will go back to her archives, but first she must visit the church and Michael's place," David suggested.

"You have fixed a meeting at the church and Michael's this afternoon, why not postpone it for today and leave it for tomorrow morning and we all should go, it will be interesting. More heads are better than one." Ayond said, collected her copies of the documents.

"And the medallion, can I have it," she looked at Sam and added, "I promise you I will not lose it.

Sam agreed and handed it over. They spent a few more moments, and parted.

# CHAPTER 10

**That night Sam talked** about his meeting with Ayond, David and Jim to Michael. He did not say anything about Ayond being an Alien, he just casually mentioned that they will be visiting his place tomorrow after the church.

"Have fun," Michael said and got up. "Tomorrow I have an early start to catch the train. See you in a couple of weeks."

Sam felt free to have the house to himself without any interference, Michael had given him full permission to do as he pleased.

The next morning, he drove the team to the church, Father Daniel was strolling when Sam's vehicle came to a screeching halt not two feet from him. He jumped back two steps and didn't look too pleased.

Ayond was first to get out of the car and went straight to Father Daniel and shook his hands. "Pleased to meet you. Heard a lot of good things about you from Sam."

She took the initiative to introduce Jim and David. After a pause, "Of course you know Sam," she said with a pinch of humour.

They walked to Father Daniel residence where they socialised and told him of their up to date position.

"Very interesting, I am sure you may find more at the Altar. I have made all the arrangement, no one will disturb us in there, say for as long as you want," Father Daniel assured.

The walked to the church. David whispered to Jim, "I have not been in one for as long as I can remember."

"Likewise, the last time was a wedding I attended ten years ago," Jim said with a giggle.

They entered by the back door. Father Daniel led the way followed by Ayond and the rest of the team in a single file. She stood in reverence and for some time looked at the Altar.

"How do you like our little church," Father Daniel asked Ayond humbly.

"I like the layout. It is unique, the figures on the pillars. Everything about it looks grandeur. It must be very old."

"The church is very old, built around the 12th century, of course it was improved upon and added a few things with the passage of time," Father Daniel led them to the Altar, with his shoulder and hands push it diagonally. It heaved gently until the well of steps appeared.

He put his hand to a switch and light fill the steps. "I fixed the lights myself, nothing fancy, but workable.

First to lead the way was Father Daniel, followed by David and Jim. Sam waited for them to reach the bottom then asked Ayond to be careful, "The steps are steep and narrow."

Gently she descended followed by Sam.

The room was brightly lit, different from the time Sam had first visited with Father Daniel using candles and hurricane lamps.

They stared at the artefacts and visually studied the room, the walls and the floor. "Can we touch some of the items," David addressed their host.

"Feel free, you can take picture if you like."

"Thank you Father, Sam had provided us copies of all this. Just studying them at first hand," David said coming close to the slate on which the child sketch was on. He picked it up and using a magnifying glass he began scrutinizing inch by inch.

"I must say the person who etched this probably used all his strength in making these impressions to make sure they last for a long time. Look at the women, she is not holding him. Her hand raised high free, as if making some kind of a gesture to a supreme leader or deity, just as in the scrolls."

Passed it on to Ayond, looked at it, said nothing and passed the slate to Jim. He too studied it minutely and said nothing.

The team was so engrossed that they did not realize two hours had passed. David broke the silence, looking at his watch, "Time flies, we better be going. Let's not keep the Reverend waiting."

"I am in no hurry. Take your time."

Shortly after they all left to Michael's house.

Parked at the front door, Ayond walked to the edge of the little garden that overlooked the village, about fifty feet below. "It is like a picture post card from here," She said.

Inside they rested for a while before descending into another abyss hosting the enigmatic objects, and the room with a tomb.

Sam led the way. They examined every item, and entered the mysterious chamber. All five stood in a semi-circle in silence stared at the tomb and chair with a crimson coloured attire resting on it.

No one spoke. Ayond hesitated, but gently moved towards the chair. She lifted the suit from its reclining position and examined it.

"Why should anyone be wearing a suit like that, I would say it is a 20th century stuff," Jim said softly.

Sam walked up and questioned, "What are these nipple like flanges for, are they inlets to the suit, to pump in air or oxygen or something?"

"You are perfectly right, Sam," Ayond put in. "Let me tell you, this gentleman must have visited a facility of ours, restricted to humans, perhaps he was taken there to show him medical facility where people are treated for blindness, contagious diseases and the like. It was a restricted area, only special persons are allowed. The date on the suit says July, 1817. One of our helpers, an Earthman disappeared with a lot of information. We looked everywhere but he just vanished. He was contaminated with a deadly disease.

"I suspect, the man buried here is that person, I wonder if the people put him there were infected. We will never know. I'll check in our files, it will be interesting to know."

Sam was thinking, "So that must be the mysterious Mr Z, All the time he was buried at Michael's. That fictitious grave out there at the cemetery was perhaps to fool the people. He was infected, must have passed it to some who touched him and fatally effected them, and that is why, the curse story was labelled to the room. Michael will be happy to know." Then with a humours tone he said, "I have a request to make. If all of us agree, I would love to meet our mysterious friend."

"I second the motion," David voice filled the room.

Sam ran out, his steps echoed as he ascended to the top to bring instruments to prow with. He returned with a couple of crowbars, a metal spade and a few miscellaneous pointed metal objects. Each one except Ayond picked an item and started to pry at the cover stone slab.

It was impossible to insert any below the cover stone that was five inches thick. After many attempts, they failed. They had to get professional to get the job done, left the room and went upstairs, exhausted.

"We can't do it, only qualified men can, and at least ten of them. But who? It would be risky to get from the outside," Sam said.

"You are right Sam, I can arrange to send a team from our organisation, if it is agreeable with you all.

"Agree." They all voiced.

"I will come with my crew tomorrow morning at ten." Ayond said.

Jim dropped them back and promised to fetch them before ten the next morning.

Sam stretched in full on the sofa and slept.

Late evening he got up and went down and spent an hour perusing through the item, and spent time examining the tomb. Took Michael father's diary went upstairs, spent the evening reading.

In bed that night he thought of how through the ages, the aliens kept in touch with their family in one form or another, sometimes losing contact but somehow, found each other again. "The guy buried down there must have been a relative, otherwise why would he come to this house. Perhaps have the answers tomorrow, and have the pleasure of meeting whoever is buried in there." With those thought he dosed off.

# CHAPTER 11

**The next day** at 10 in the morning Ayond arrived with ten men. All looked very athletic, with stern expressionless faces. They formed a straight line, queued into the house, led by Ayond, ignored Sam's polite ushering.

Some carried thick ropes and some had strange looking metallic objects. They placed all their equipment at one side of the room. Positioned a tripod with a glass bowl on top, lit and hummed with continuous whining sound, encircled the slab with ropes, and began to heave. Ayond explained to Sam the function of the tripod. "It creates a diffused vibrations which loosens the cover from the main body. The men have to pull hard to get off."

It gently slid off and rested on one side of the tomb. "Easy to slide it back when we have done with our exhumation. They will wait upstairs," Ayond said and asked the men to leave.

The whole operation lasted less than twenty minutes. Ayond and Sam just stared at the coffin. They were interrupted by the arrival of David, Jim and Father Daniel.

"Forgive us we are late, got caught in the traffic," David apologized.

"You are just in time. Meet our friend, and surprisingly a blood relation of Sam, Michael and Daniel. Last night I went through centuries old archives. He was the direct descendent of the person who buried his father in 1164 and had no issues, and buried that box.

"I was confused as to how his lineage continued as he had no children. But then I found the answer. We the aliens chose a wife for him from our specie. He was one of the brothers from that lineage, Nanook was his code name given by us. He was buried in the house by his uncle.

The letter N was tattooed on his on his right hand which also had a code number to operate freely within our facilities. He should be carrying a cube which has special features. Only we can operate it. We had lost track of him when he was on a mission, and that was the last of our communications with your family." Ayond concluded with a smile looking at Sam.

Sam said very softly, "What a story. No one would believe it. We are the lucky ones. The box we were looking for must have been buried with him, most probably somewhere on his person, and the initial on his hand is not a Z but an N, for Nanook.

"All the official records on this guy were falsely entered. That relative of ours, must have had some influence to get it done. Well, let's get the suspense over with and meet with our deceased relative."

Sam was the first to jump into the pit, followed by David. Father Daniel made the sign of the cross and lifting his attire waist up, joined in.

Jim and Ayond stood looking down at the coffin. Sam began to peel off the lid. It gave way, a plank was lifted off and the rest crumbled and fell on the skeleton. Gently he lifted it and put it at one side.

From his tightly gripped skeletal palm, Sam extracted a cube, muddy and unrecognizable.

They studied the skeleton from head to toe and found nothing else.

Sam handed the cube to Ayond and said to her, "I think we should get him covered and let him rest in peace. He has done his job."

He studied the skeleton again from head to toe and found nothing. "Must have stripped naked at burial. Burnt all his clothes, save the crimson suit," Sam observed.

She asked Sam to call the waiting crew to put the lid back on the tomb.

"I will see if the cube is still functional, and what it says, I will go back with my men, call you tomorrow." Ayond said and parted.

David got up from the sofa and like a teacher in a classroom he paced the room and spoke. "Gentlemen, we have put ourselves in the jaws of an unknown predicament. Imagine us being involved with Aliens, how are we going to handle the situation. Are they what they seem, friendly or use us to harm our fellow beings.

"We have no choice, I don't think Ayond is the sort, let us wait and see, and what she has in store for us. We have stumbled on something that remained dormant for more than eight centuries, and now this gentleman. We have penetrated areas that would

74

have been folk tales or legends, and now we are literally active actors in that fiasco.

"Whatever is the outcome, it is going to be fun, and, we may be catapulted into fame and headline news."

# CHAPTER 12

**For two days** there was no news from Ayond. It was late afternoon on the third day that she called.

"Hello Sam, got a little busy, couldn't call, regarding the cube, it was given to Nanook to trace the medallion, but we now know that it was buried with his father by his son who had no issues.

"As I had mentioned, my predecessors in order not to lose that son who had no issues, got him married to one of us, he was blessed with a son from that marriage, apparently he had forgotten his commitment to his father, and the metal box he had buried; as a result the medallion was lost. He should have retrieved them. That was not to be. Interestingly, what I found; from that lineage, you, Michael and Daniel are direct descendants, from one of Nanook's brothers, going back to the twelfth century."

"Unbelievable, do mean to say that we have alien blood in us." Sam said excitedly.

"Yes Sam, alien blood. I have always suspected that there was something special about you."

"Thank you, Michael and Daniel will flip over when I tell them."

"Sam, can you get your team to meet me on Sunday, about noon, I will give you the address when you confirm their acceptance."

Sam wasted no time. He was back on the phone to Ayond within the hour.

"The address is simple," she made him write it down, "Once you reach that spot, you will see a large black iron gate with a gold lion's head design in its middle. It is an empty plot. Dead opposite to it, is where we are. Someone at the gate will meet you."

On Sunday, Sam picked David, Jim and Father Daniel and arrived at the spot. Parked their vehicle in front of the Iron Gate with the lion's head. Opposite to that, there was no structure of any kind, just an empty ground with a small gate. No sign of life anywhere, then a man appeared at the gate, which opened with a squeak, and walked up to them.

"Good day gentlemen, please leave your car here, and follow me. They walked through the small gate that squeaked, and across some fifty feet on barren terrain, entered into what looked like a wooden shack.

They exchanged glances not believing what they were seeing. Their escort led them through a narrow passage, at the end of it, opened a door with a flight of stairs hardly four feet wide. At the end of it there was a metal door. He placed his palm against it, and politely said, "I leave now, someone will receive you," He said and started his ascend back.

The metallic door slid open, a voice, through a microphone requested them to enter. They did, and were greeted by a brightly lit hall and saw a figure approach them from a distance with hands waving. They recognised Ayond's voice, "Welcome my friends. It is a great pleasure to have you here." She shook hands, and led them to what looked like an elevator. Moments later, they emerged into a larger hall, at one end were windows overlooked into a garden with bright sunshine.

"Are we back again to the surface?" Sam asked.

"No Sam, we are fifty feet underground, and that 'sunshine' is artificial light." At the end of the hall, stopped in front of a wall. She pressed her palm against it and a door slid open, exposing a room like a five star hotel, with chairs, some small table and a glass cupboard full of bottles and several glasses. Two attendants stood next to it.

"Make yourselves comfortable gentlemen, we shall have some tea or coffee before we start." She signalled the attendants and they got to work.

"Quite a place you have down here, why underground? It is cheaper to build up there." David started the conversation.

"Cost is not a factor, privacy and secrecy is the main issue. Remember we are aliens, guests on your planet. We don't want to disturb anybody nor do we want to be disturbed." After a pause, she continued, "I am so glad you could make it, will work to gather with open arms, nothing will be hidden away from you and treated as one of us."

That statement by Ayond relaxed the air of uncertainty in the visitor's mind.

"The preliminaries of this venture requires us to meet constantly, at least for a couple of weeks, if not more. Soon you will know the importance of this mission, it would not be convenient for you to come and go, so we decided to host you and live with us. Alternatively, we can arrange transportation on daily basis to bring you to our facility, but that would be cumbersome. How about moving in for this period, think about it."

Sam looked at David, then at Jim and Father Daniel. "What says you, I personally think it is a good idea to move in."

David promptly replied, "I am in for it, if we are to take this whole affair seriously we better be here. I am single and have no responsibilities, both my sons are on their own, well settled."

"Count me in," Jim said softly then added, "I have to ring up the wife and make an excuse. As far as the shop is concerned business is down and my sons are in France, no harm in shutting it down temporarily."

"What about you Father?" Sam asked softly.

"Sam, it is difficult for me. Can't close down the Church. What I will do is to go back and arrange for someone to run it while I am away. I should be back in three days' time. I will call when ready, send me a transport to fetch me."

"I will arrange for a car to bring you, and when you are ready, just call me."

"Sam, I take it that you have accepted our invitation."

"Gladly," was his prompt respond.

"Jim you can either go to your wife or use the phone."

"I will use the phone."

"I am so glad with your decisions, let me take you to your rooms," She said getting up. They walked through a maze of corridors, stopped at door with a number on it. "This is room number 1, the others next to it go up to 10. David this will be yours, and the rest can chose on your own. She handed each a ring. "Put it on, it is the key to enter your rooms, just point it on the point of light on your door and will allow you enter. Watch this," she said and pointer David's ring to the light. The door slid open.

They entered, from a table picked a little object, "With this you can switch on and off the lights, draw the curtains, switch on your television and call room service. Instructions are on it. Pointed to a corner where a slim cupboard with glass on three sides, a dim light exposed what looks like alcoholic beverages and cans of soft drinks. "And at that corner is the bed," she said and walked up, and pressed a button on the wall. A luxurious bed peeled off. "Press again, it will it will retract back.

"And by the way, you can step out into the garden, and enjoy the flowers and sunshine." Pointed to a large glass windows exposing a lush green orchard.

"One more thing," Ayond added, "There is a little formality we have to do. I have to take you to our Guardian and Supreme High to introduce you. They are the big bosses and heads of the facility. They are the be all and end all, nobody questions or disobey them. They can be very harsh if provoked and but gentle at all times.

"Once that is out of the way, we can do anything you like. Go through our archives, record books, films and shows, and our contributions to the human race."

Ayond waited for any questions that may be asked. No one spoke.

"Good, first we meet the Guardian. I had briefed him about our project and he is more than thrilled to see that we succeed. He had informed the Supreme High and he too was pleased. Just a note of caution, please do not question the Supreme High or make sudden gesture, he is very sensitive and can react very violently.

"He is the gentlest and can be the cruellest. That is why we call him the Supreme High. There is nothing above him as far as we are concerned.

"Now let's go and have some more refreshments before we meet the bosses. We have some time to spare, a cup of tea wold be refreshing." She said as they walked out into a corridor, and entered what looked like a staff cafeteria. When they saw Ayond, the chatter stopped and stood up. She waved a hand and put them at ease.

Seeing this Sam and the rest realised that Ayond had some authority, tea and some refreshments were served, and after while left.

Entered an elevator. Inside, she said something to it, flashes of green and yellow lights encompassed them, shortly after, replace by a flood of green.

"Please stand still and don't move a muscle." She requested.

David, Jim and Sam looked at each other, quizzically.

Just then a beam of red light hit every person, including Ayond. Scanned each individual from head to toe, only then the elevator door opened.

There were two persons to greet them. They were dressed in crimson suits, with a hood covering the entire head. It reminded Sam of the orange suite found in Michael's house. "So our mysterious cousin buried there must have worn a similar outfit while working with the aliens."

They were taken to a room and to every body's surprise they were made to dress in the same attire as their attendants, except Ayond. They all remembered the orange suit and were thinking the same as Sam's first impression.

A green light flashed on their heads. Then with a polite gesture one of the attendants asked them to follow her in a single file. They entered a room, left the attendants outside. Ayond picked up a small gadget that looked like a ruler.

She waved it from left to right. For a few seconds nothing happened. A voice asked Ayond to put her left hand against the door. After a few seconds there was a gentle click almost inaudible. The door slid open. Ayond walked in and invited her guest.

She led them through a narrow passage. At one point a voice told them to stop. They did. A beam of blue light scanned each person.

A young female dressed in normal skirt and blouse, and wore black boots greeted them. Then moved to Sam, "I am guessing, can't recognise you in that attire, you must be Sam, who visited our shop in London."

Instant recognition by Sam, "You have grown to be beautiful lady,"

With a blush on her face, she said softly, "Thank you Sam."

Ayond stepped forward, "Can we leave the chatter for later and get down to business."

"Sorry, please follow me," the girl said.

"Tell me your name," Sam said softly and took the lead to follow her.

She did not response fearing Ayond's reprisal.

They reached a wall, she waved the ruler shaped gadget and the wall split open. Ayond walked in first, followed by the girl. The rest were ushered in with a polite gesture of the hand. The wall shut behind them with a gentle click. A streak of light flashed across the entire wall.

"Gentlemen, we are now in the Guardian's chamber," Ayond said softly.

They looked around and saw nothing in the dimly lit room.

"Please follow me," the young girl said leading them to the front of the room. They stopped in front of an elevated pedestal on which there were seven empty chairs. They exchanged glances not seeing any person or persons sitting on them. They stood in silence staring at the pedestal.

"Look something is happening," David whispered.

A haze of blue light began to cover the chairs, then it began to collect on to the centre seat. When the haze disappeared they saw a tall gentleman dressed in a black robe.

They were relaxed to see a normal human looking gentleman, "A handsome young man, but something odd about his facial texture. It is more metallic than normal skin," David observed.

"What a shiny cranium he has," Jim pondered.

A voice from somewhere requested them to go up to the pedestal and sit down. They did with Ayond and the girl leading, sat on either side of the Guardian, and with the rest filled the remaining ones.

There was silence for a couple of minutes.

The Guardian stood up, and in a gentle baritone voice he spoke.

"Sam, David, Daniel and Jim, I welcome you to our facility. I have been told all about you. We have made a complete check, especially on Sam, Daniel and Michael who have a special place with us.

"How special, Ayond must have told you. But for now, all of you will be treated, not as guest, but part and parcel of this facility. You will in due course study our books and teach you the knowledge that no human being had the privilege. This is important for the success of our mission on Earth and the survival of life on this planet.

"You have something that belonged to us. It was lost for many centuries due to our negligence. The medallion that was carefully buried by one of your ancestors was a responsible act by him as he thought that he had no issues to pass it on, he buried it, soon after he was married to a women of our choice and had a child, and forgot to pass on what his father instructed, perhaps he was mesmerised by his wife's beauty that his faculties were jeopardized. We hold no grudge against him as the medallion is now back with us." He said with a humorous note.

"Sam, Michael and Daniel are the direct descendants of that person. As for now, we have a lot of work to do. Soon I will meet with you again to follow on your progress. You have the capable hands of Ayond to assist you, meanwhile, go and meet our Supreme High who awaits to meet you. After that, you will not need the cumbersome attire you are waring, as you will be cleared of all obligations."

The blue haze once again filled the pedestal and he was gone.

Ayond and the girl came down and without saying a word. The rest followed.

Went to another section of the room and waited. The girl said something to the ruler she was holding. The ruler lit up, then began to blink. She gave a command and once again it lit up brightly. The wall in front of them began to slide open. She was the first to enter followed by Ayond. The room was almost dark, they were assured in, soon a canopy of golden haze of light began to envelope them. When it faded away, they were astonished to see the colour of their suits had changed to the colour of gold.

Ayond whispered, "Do not speak unless spoken to."

The dimly lit room, began to gradually light up, in front of them they could see clearly a cube, five feet high, with several little square and round windows in which active hands and flickering lights constantly played.

Within the cube, faint churnings, the little windows narrowed, and shut, replaced by pin size lights all over its facial structure.

A voice filled the room, not knowing where it was coming from, the team was confused and looked around to locate the source. Ayond looked at them and shook her head and with a gentle gesture to look in front.

The voice said, "Welcome to the sons of the great ones and their friends. I have known your lineage for more than two millenniums, from the time Amelhop your first ancestor who served us and was a priest in an Egyptian temple we helped to build, for a high priestess. She was one of us, or better still created by us."

Sam was confused as to what he meant, so were the others.

"Nothing to be confused about," the voice continued as if he had read their minds.

Their thoughts went wilder. "How on earth did he know what were we thinking," David mind was not at ease.

"You all are mere humans, cannot visualize the abilities of a machine and the people who built it. That was many years ago when man on Earth was living in caves. Now please listen to me very attentively."

Sam and the rest realized that they were talking to a highly advanced computer, but it was much more than that, like a living being, with the skill to read minds. "Better control my thoughts, he knows everything. This is embarrassing," Sam was thinking.

"Sam, you are right, do not be embarrassed, most of us are fallible. In due course, all the bumpiness will be smoothed out. In my case, after many trials and errors, my makers had perfected the ultimate machine, if you want to call me that. I am complete, but not a God as you humans may think me to be. I am here to guide the human race which, in my opinion is going astray, and bring doom to their doorstep.

"For many years our message had been misunderstood, instead of following our instruction to be good, instead, branded us as Gods to be worship and in return, asked us to bless them with good harvests and wealth, they wanted us to do their job. Humans in general are good, but a good number are lazy, selfish, and love to accumulate wealth, to the extent of inflicting harm to others. In some other lands, people have understood our message and followed our teachings, though not fully." The Supreme High stopped, then added, "Forgive me for expressing such thoughts, and as far as you are concerned, we found you all to be good recipients to understand our ways."

Again there was a pause, "You live in a world of confused minds, in due course when ignorance is conquered, truth will prevail. But then it might be too late.

"For now, we must end this meeting and give you enough time to digest what we talked about. I will meet you again very soon," The voice said and gradually the lights began fade. Ayond and the girl led them out, and into the main hall leading to David's room.

They all sat at random on the chairs that were placed casually, the girl went to a glass cupboard and took out some glasses. "The bar is open gentlemen, place your orders," she said in an inviting tone almost musical.

David was first to speak, "I'll have a double scotch on the rocks."

Followed almost simultaneously by the others. They all ordered the same. "Well, in that case I'll have one too," Ayond said raising a hand at the bar tender.

The drinks were served and they settled down. For a few moments only the sound of ice being shaken in the beautifully designed heavy crystal glass. After a few sips David spoke, "That was unbelievable. Imagine that computer was talking to us as if it was a person. On top of that, it also read our minds." He took a large gulp of his whiskey and then quaffed the entire glass. "That was good," getting up from his chair and handing the glass to the girl, "One more please."

Jim shyly murmured a few words, "From what I have seen, I think we humans are completely illiterate compared to that thing."

Ayond promptly corrected him, "Excuse me Jim that 'thing' as you put it, and you David referring to the Supreme High as an 'it', is not a machine, but an all knowing entity, much higher than you and I, as far as we are concerned. I don't mean to be rude, perhaps it was just the way you phrased your sentences. However, it was something new to all of you. You will get used to us in time, especially when we get deeper into our project. You will have to forget living in your world, you all are special to be part of us, just like a few others before you, but that was long ago.

"Yes Sam," his hand was raised, "To me it was not a surprise, perhaps I read too many Si-fi novels, and have always believed that someday what we consider as fiction will be facts. Man's progress was slow in the past, but suddenly in the twentieth century doors opened and the twenty-first shall open more doors, leading humanity to higher pedestals."

Ayond did not response immediately, she was thinking, "I know what he means," but decided not to pursue. She turned to Father Daniel, "You are quiet, perhaps nursing your drink."

He shuffled in his chair and looked at the rest one by one. In a preacher like sermon he began. "I don't know how to put it, but in all His wisdom God had provide incredible knowledge to His creations, like your making of the Supreme High."

Ayond interrupted, "Correction, we did not make the Supreme High, he was already there, found him eons ago on a planet the size a little bigger than your moon, all alone in a structure made of an unknown metal. There was no life on the planet. It was green with waterfalls, the only planet in a binary system.

"In brief I will tell you how he happened to be with us. The credit goes to the Guardian, who by sheer coincidence landed on our world. He told us that he was robot, highly intelligent with exceptional capabilities such as travel in space by turning his bodily structure to light waves or photons and the list goes on. However, he and many like him were made by people like you and I, they were to do manual and administrative jobs to fill the gap of their declining race due to a freak natural catastrophe, a rainfall that has turned all living beings and to some extent plants, sterile.

"As the population dwindled the need for robots and androids became essential. Then they build a super machine and with its help created a highly sophisticated computer, it could think for itself, create new ideas and machines. It was then, they, with the help of this super computer built the Guardians. When the population died away, there was no use for the Guardians or any other machine, the super computer asked them to store him in a safe location and all of them should go out and seek planets where they can be useful.

"It was this Guardian, whom you all met today, who came to our world, and with his help retrieved the super computer, and because of his ineffable knowledge and capabilities, we gave him the title of Supreme High."

"But why credit him so highly above your people, is there no one more capable in your world?" Jim asked.

"Good question, the answer is none. Why? Because when our world was jettisoned out our binary system due to a tug of war between the two suns, and our planet began to drift into space as a rouge planet, He had full control of its magnetic field and weather, sailing us comfortably into the void of space until we found your solar system.

"By the way, at the time we found him, people on Earth were apelike primates, so you can evaluate the level of the technology within him at that period of time. Of course, I was not born then, it was very much earlier before my time. I born on Earth only recently. Enough of my talking, how about some more refreshment to satiate my throat?"

There was a pin drop silence as they were dazed by her amazing narration about the Guardian and Supreme High. Perhaps no one paid attention to her request for a drink. It was David who got up and looked at the blank their faces, with a loud voice he broke the stillness, "Anyone to join me?"

"David, you didn't hear me, I said I was thirsty," Ayond exclaimed loud and clear.

Soon the bar was crowded and someone shouted, "Cheers, to happy days to come."

David took Ayond aside, "I can't imagine what we have learnt today. We are living in a different world, in a different time."

"Yes David, both the Guardian and the Supreme High are a wonder, the ingenuity of the people who created them, a *lifeform*, if you allow me to use that word, far superior than their own. One more thing, at times you will find them more humane than you would think."

Sam waited for the rest to take their seats then popped a question to the girl, whom he met at the antique shop, almost in a whisper, "Now tell me, what is your name?" He looked back at Ayond, she was busy talking to Father Daniel.

"Aishtra," she whispered.

"That is an odd name, but it is beautiful, what does it mean."

"In our language it means, 'the gift of life'."

Ayond got up from her chair, "I think we had enough today. I leave you in peace to ponder over what you have learnt, by the way talk among yourselves freely, good or bad, the rooms are not bugged, and we have nothing to fear from you. You all have passed the test of loyalty," Ayond assured them and before she left she turned to Sam, "You can have your chit chat later on with Aishtra as you know her name now."

Sam stared at Ayond thinking, "She knows about our conversation, nothing is secret in this place."

She looked at him and smiled and turned to Father Daniel, "Aishtra will arrange your transport to the church, and tell the driver when to bring you back to the facility.

Ayond left the room with a wave of her hand and Aishtra requested Father Daniel to go along with her.

# CHAPTER 13

**Three days later** Father Daniel retuned wearing a trousers and a push shirt. He was holding a brief case.

"Father you look smart in that attire, what's in the brief case," Sam said with a grin.

"Just clothes."

"You don't need them. While you were away, we had a tailor who made us some beautiful outfits suitable to the environment we are in, he will make some for you too," Sam explained.

"You must be joking," Father Daniel thought Sam must be teasing him.

Minutes later, a visitor accompanied by Aishtra walked in.

Sam announced in a theatrical fashion, "Father, get ready to be measured, this gentleman is your tailor."

David stepped forward and asked them to sit down. Then addressed Father Daniel, "We were all and measured, now it is your turn."

They watched. The tailor began his performance, of measuring the subject's length and breadth, lifting of the arms and gauging of the legs, Daniels acrobatic movements were more like a ballet dancer performing a ritual dance. A grin on the onlooker's faces developed into a bust of laughter. Daniel looked back at them, not amused. The tailor left shortly after.

David raised his hand, "As we are all here, want to say something, I have been thinking of the situation we are in. How fortunate we are to be in this position, it is unbelievable, like being in a science fiction novel. God knows, how it will end. Can't believe that we are at the headquarters of an alien base, and how many like this do they have. Perhaps they are in touch with Presidents, Prime Ministers and scientist, but that is not our concern. As long as we are being treated as equals and with respect, we should not have any problem.

"The medallion is the key in all this. What it is and where it will be used. Perhaps it has a message of some kind to lead to a hidden artefact or even a treasure. How will it affect the world and the human race as a whole? These are few questions, I am at a loss. I want you all to think seriously."

Father Daniel shuffled in his chair and put in softly, "I have served the All Mighty and shut my eyes to all around me. We have been told what the scientist have been talking about like the Big Bang and other findings about the Universe as false, goes against religious beliefs, just 'accept' blindly what is said in the Book. No deviation, until kingdom come."

There was a long pause, crossed himself, and continued. They listened attentively and waited.

"Now we are talking to people from another world and what I have seen made me think otherwise. For millions of years they have survived and reached great heights, what made them tick?

"Why don't they come out openly to the world outside and benefit mankind with the truth of how we came to be and are we on the right path?"

David took the floor, "They cannot. There will be social upheaval. Chaos of untold level, people will not only be confused but too early to grasp, through time, when ignorance has been outlawed, only then, the light of wisdom will outweigh the inevitable. The Reverend has made a point. What I suggest is that for now, we just go along with whatever Ayond tells us to do and be genuinely involved. Do you all agree?"

They all agreed with one voice.

"Why don't you all go to your rooms and show Daniel his, meanwhile if you all don't mind I am going to have a nap, let's meet in two hours in my room."

They were back at David's room at the appointed time. The telephone rang, Sam answered. "This is Ayond, see you in half an hour." She hung up.

Shortly after she arrived with Aishtra, both were dressed in a typical formal evening outfit.

"What a transformation from the ladies a few hours ago. They are more human than alien," whispered Jim to Sam.

"Shush, they may hear you," Sam said quietly and with a loud voice greeted their guests, "Welcome and please come in. You both look lovely, out of this world."

"Thank you Sam, you all may escort us to dinner," Ayond said

"You will have to show us the way," Sam came forward and put his arm around hers leading the way.

The dining room was not too large, just about four tables, with a large one to one side.

On the larger tables two candle stands and six chairs. Ayond sat at the head, on one side Sam and Daniel, on the opposite, David, Aishtra and Jim.

David started to converse with Ayond, "Not many people here, it's practically empty."

"This room is for seniors, there is another room for workers and junior staff," she replied.

They socialized and on many occasions David's laughter filled the room. Sam kept looking at Aishtra, but avoided long eye contact for fear of Ayond's perusing glances.

Father Daniel suggested that he should be called by his name without the prefix 'Father.' Sam was most delighted and raised a toast, "Welcome to the club of mortals, Cousin Daniel."

Daniel raised his glass and put in politely, "Just call me Daniel, forget the word cousin also," looking at Sam.

Ayond raised her glass, "That is very brave of you, that gesture will put us more at ease. After all we are one happy family."

"Cheers!" Daniel said with a loud voice.

After dinner, the conversation continued, with joy and laughter.

Ayond looked at her watch, "It is getting late, please excuse us, we'll meet tomorrow, about noon. Before going to their respective rooms they assembled at David's for a night cap. He suggested they meet in his room for breakfast.

# CHAPTER 14

**They met at** ten in the morning. David was in his pyjamas. "Come in, I will take a few minutes, meanwhile you can help yourselves to some orange juice. The maid just brought it in."

Breakfast was served out in the garden. Sam started, "Our meeting with Ayond today will perhaps explain many things. We'll have to behave business like and professional. Perhaps she will tell us more about themselves and the facility we are in."

"That will be fascinating, I want to know which part of the universe they come from," Jim said.

"And if there are more planets with people," Daniel add.

"We'll have to wait and see, if she does not bring the issue then we can ask. We should not burden her with too many questions." Sam suggested.

"We should just listen and ask may be a couple of questions," David advised.

"What a view we have out here, well-manicured plants, the colourful flowers of so many shades, and to top it all the bright artificial sun light like sitting somewhere outside in a luxurious home.

Breakfast was served, leisurely they eat, and while having their tea, David looked at his watch, "It is almost mid-day, Ayond should be here any minute.

He had hardly finished, when Ayond and Aishtra entered.

"Enjoying the comforts of your hospitality," David said appreciably.

"Take you time and finish your breakfast, we are in no hurry," Ayond said and sat down.

Minutes later, they left the room, Ayond explained the schedule for day. "We will just familiarise you with the facility and something about us." Sam looked at David and Jim and exchanged glances.

They entered a room with a large screen perched on the wall. On a large conference table, pads and pens well placed in front of each chair.

"It is like an executive's business meeting," David remarked.

"Make yourselves comfortable, sit where you please. I will sit at the head of the table with Aishtra to my right.

They sat and waited for Ayond to say speak.

"Any questions you want to ask before I start," she said.

David promptly replied before any could say anything, "No mam, we would like to listen," exchanging glances with the rest.

"Very well, let's start." The screen lit up. A globe appeared. It was a planet, not the Earth. One large continent, filled nearly one half of the planet's surface. Rounded on the top and elongated at the bottom, with a blue ocean all around it.

"That is our world, or was our world, how we miss it," she said with a sigh and emotion. "I had spoken to you earlier about our planet but now we have visual. By the way, I also mentioned to you that I was born on Earth, but all the same, it was my ancestral home.

"It was a rogue planet. You may not have heard the term 'rogue', it is a plant that have gone astray. Our world is twice as old as Earth. We had six planets, three are bigger than your Jupiter and three about the size of Earth. Only ours had life, the rest were uninhabitable, either too close to our suns or too far. Our world was a little smaller than Earth. Spinning very slowly, its rotation was seventy two hours, green with a lot of water and plenty of rainfall. Animal species in millions, people just one race, like me," she paused for a few second, turned to Aishtra and she nodded to Ayond, pausing for several seconds, then with a smile on her face, "Aishtra comes from your Earth, not one of us.

She allowed a full minute for them to digest that revelation. All exchanged glances, they looked confused.

"But," Sam could not hold himself, "We thought she is one of you, not a human."

"She is not," Ayond replied casually.

More confusion on their faces. "But you said she is human," David broke in.

"I never said she was human, I said she is from Earth."

More confused faces, David could not take it, "You talk in riddles, please stop joking, how is she from Earth and not human?"

"That is exactly what I said, she is an Earth specie not known to you but in some places in your world, know of them. In fact some can communicate and meet with them. This species are known as Jinn in the Arab world.

"I never heard of them, unless, you mean what we call demons or spirits, are they the Jinn?" Jim asked.

Ayond looked at Aishtra, "You are more qualified to explain."

She pressed a button on a key board and a picture appeared on the screen. A male figure appeared looked just like a common man standing next to a lamp post. The next picture showed his face only.

"Look at the eyes, see anything special?" She said bringing the picture close showing the eyes.

"The pupil is a straight line, not round like us?" Jim said with a questioning tone. Then added, "All this time we have been meeting you, and none of us noticed it."

They got up from their chairs and one by one examined Aishtra's eyes.

Sam, came very close almost touching her face with his and stared for along minute. "I like them," he said and sat down.

"That is the main difference in our physical appearance, besides, we have the ability to take any shape, as an animal, a male or an inanimate object. Our origin goes many billion years ago when the world was in its infancy. Lightening and electromagnetic displays were ruling the planet and methane was falling as rain. In a nut shell that was the period when life began to form, developing into a specie compatible with the climatic conditions of the time. I can go on and on but to make it brief, millions of years later we emerged as a race capable of travelling with the speed of light."

They listened with wonder, some had their mouths open, no one said anything waited for her to finish.

"We go into space, we don't need air, and we are made of electric particles. Some of us can be naughty, go after men or woman of the human race. In facts some of us married humans and some helped mankind in many ways," She paused then added, "That is my story, any questions?"

Ayond looked at their faces who were stunned by Aishtra's revelation.

"I have a question for you," Daniel was the first to speak.

"Why I have not seen any of you, as you say that you are all over everywhere. No mention of you all in any of our Books?"

"Simple, you may have met some of us, as I said we can take the shape of humans in a variety of forms, and how many times have you looked closely into their eyes. Besides we are very well mentioned in the Holy Book of the Islamic Faith."

"I have a question," David interrupted, "How are you all connected with extra-terrestrial or Ayond and her people."

"We are not working with extra-terrestrials only I happen to and that is by accident. When I was a little girl, my parents and I were traveling in one of our space ships just above the Earth over England when we had a major accident, our ship crashed and my parents died. I survived. I managed to get out of the craft badly bruised and had a few fractures.

"Luckily a woman came to my rescue. She took me to a house where she treated my wounds. A few days later I was in a better condition and the woman introduced herself as Ayond. Our spaceship was hovering near their facility, and when it crashed they came to investigate and found me. They took me and brought me up as one of them and here I am. The spaceship was taken away by Ayond's people."

"Fascinating story," Sam said, "you have not tried to contact the Jinn to take you back home?"

"It was decided not to, that would have exposed the presence of Ayond's people which they did not want to for their reasons, and if they have seen the crash they must have assumed that we all were dead. I am very happy here, Ayond is like a mother to me and because of her I have reached to this position."

Daniel was absorbed in deep thought, still trying to figure out what the Jinn are. The west has regarded them as demons or evil spirits.

He looked at Ayond and began softly, "Why is it that our knowledge is so distorted. I am beginning to see a different picture of the world around us. We are really still living in an age of ignorance. Many things are hidden away from us perhaps to suit those who rule and control us."

Ayond realized as to where the discussions may lead to. She put in very gently, looking at Daniel, "In a way you may be right, but we'll leave it at that for the time being. I will resume where Aishtra left off, she is the only Jinn working with us, but there are also some humans. We recruited them young from orphanages and broken homes. You may have seen some of them in the dining room and elsewhere in the facility, their earthly behaviour and style have changed. They are now part of our culture so to speak.

"This facility is the headquarters of all our bases on Earth. It is very old about 5000 years, before that it was located in Italy and before that in the Middle East. We keep changing our location to suit the time. Many thousand years ago, when we first landed, it was in the Indus Valley, what is now Pakistan."

Jim interrupted by putting in gently, "I wonder where you will move, next?"

Ayond looked at him and replied, "Depending on the world situation, cannot say. But what I can say, is that we are very comfortable where we are. The authorities understand us well, and were allowed to build our facilities to house our spaceships and our people."

"You have spaceships?" Sam asked.

"Yes Sam, we use them sparingly. Our main policy is not to interfere in your politics and wars. Only on certain situations, only on some errands when the Supreme High or the Guardian commands it. I will not get into that, perhaps another time."

David raised a question, "You said you are comfortable here, how much the authorities know of your activities and why are they are giving a blind eye to what you do?"

"We explained to them who we are. We are here on Earth many thousands of years ago when man was emerging as a spices as we know them today. That has given us the right to enjoy the beauty of your planet." She explained.

# CHAPTER 15

"**Let me continue** from where we left of earlier, "About 16,000 thousand years ago by your calendar our planet began to misbehave, its rotation began to slow down and wobble gently, and slowly without having any serious effect on us. The two suns in our system were having a tug of war with our planet in between, ultimately it slipped away, began to drift into space, surprisingly the planet continued to spin normally, the atmosphere held by its gravity, everything was normal, a unique situation. We thought we were going to die in space, we asked the Supreme High about our predicament. He just said, 'Go about your work as if nothing has happened, I have fixed the planet's axis and corrected its gravitational stress. It will continue to sail in space for eternity unless it hits another planet or fall into a sun.' There are many such rouge planets and even suns that keep on drifting."

The screen showed briefly scenes of their drift in space. They were interrupted by attendants bringing in some refreshments.

Tea and coffee were served with some sandwiches. No one talked, the sandwiches devoured mercilessly. Soon they were settled at the table and waited attentively for Ayond to continue.

The screen lit up. "Now you will see our planet floating freely in space. We set up three satellites, one to monitor our path in space, the other two to keep an eye on our atmosphere and land mass.

"Miraculously we were in perfect shape and continued to drift but our rotation was getting slower and slower, the day light from our suns were fading fast, soon we had no light. The rotation stopped, weather was getting nasty, and it was too cold and dark. Ice began to develop at the poles, gradually began to spread on to the continent, a period of an ice age crippled our life, now look at the screen."

Dark space, with the planet surface filled with countless dots of light of homes, more or less showing the shape of the continent. "Just to remind you, our planet had one landmass," Ayond pointed out. Then something dramatic happened. One side of the planet suddenly lit up. A powerful light from a satellite, like an artificial moon, beamed on to the planet. "After a long and hard work we managed to put it up, of course with the assistance of the Supreme High." Ayond was interrupted by a remark by Sam, "Unbelievable, what would you have done without him?

"We would have been tumbling in space with the loss of all life and ultimately fall free like an asteroid," She replied, "But that did not happen. The heat from the satellite had no effect of the accumulating ice, the cold was unbearable, many lives were lost, we had to build shelters underground. We were on the brink of doom."

"How did you finally come to Earth?" David resting his head on his palm said in a low voice.

"It was a miracle when we spotted your solar system, and were heading toward your moon. Close enough to it, gave us chance to get into our spaceships and head for your planet. We carried as many people as we could, in total, about 100,000, the rest were left behind to meet their fate. Just then, the planet began to wobble and shake, destroying nearly all communication and other infrastructures, leaving the planet future hopelessly bleak.

"Those left behind was regrettable, but could not be helped, we were certain that our world will either get drawn to the sun and plunge into it or sail on to an unknown destination.

"We had no idea of what had happened to them. A few hundreds of years later when we were well settled on Earth and sent our ships and probed to survey areas of the solar system, we spotted our planet comfortably settled between Jupiter and Saturn. We deduced it was caught by the sun and put it into orbit. It takes just over twelve years to orbit.

"Somehow, the saviours manged to rebuild the basic infrastructures, set up communication and sun reflectors to enhance its heating effect, to us here on Earth, was a joyous news. We sent ships to communicate with them, but told us to stay away, they were unhappy as we had left their ancestors behind. We took a brave decision to land, they asked our mission of competent negotiators to leave, but after a reasonable manoeuvres of words and explanations, they finally forgave us, in return we offered to revitalize the planet by taking the Supreme High to advice with the Guardian to remain and supervise the operations.

"They told the Guardian that at the time when they had settled in orbit, their living conditions were beyond hope of survival, it was a surprise when some ships landed, and explained that they come from one of the moons of a large planet, they did not specify which one, and were friendly and helped build our underground homes. They also said, that some of their kind live on the third planet from the sun and the first to evolve there before any other living beings."

She stopped and got up from her chair. "Gentlemen that ends our session for today. You have learnt a lot about us. More in due course."

Before you go, I want to ask Aishtra a question, David pleaded. "How about telling us a little more about your people and where you live?"

"I have already mentioned to you, we are like humans but with special gifts, like appearing and disappearing, travel physically at high speed, we live here on Earth, most of our homes are below and above the surface, in what you might term as a different dimension.

"There are Jinn similar to us in other parts of the solar system as Ayond had explained, mostly on some of the moons of Jupiter and Saturn. They and we have technologically advanced in all fields of science and in the so called flying saucers. They and we are watching your progress, especially in space. Fearing that you bring in war and disease and pollute our habitats we kept an eye on your space activities. That is all for now, more next time."

"Do we look aggressive to you," Sam said with a tinge of humour

"Not you all, I wish the people as a whole were like you, we would have contacted you and helped you technologically. Perhaps sometime in the future."

"Just one more question, how many sexes do you have," Jim asked.

"Two, like you humans and behave and misbehave also like you."

Daniel was itching to ask the touchy subject of religion, he shuffled in his seat and stood up, "You don't have to answer this question, do have a God?"

Aishtra promptly answered him, "Your God is our God too."

"Thank you." Daniel decided not to go any further, seeing Ayond's uneasy facial expression.

To change the subject, David said getting up, "That was a splendid morning, we are humbly indebted to Ayond and you, for the information and knowledge given to us."

"You shall have many more," she replied.

They walked out, with Ayond and Aishtra accompanying, they entered the dining room. They were served a purple drink. "This is from a special fruit grown in our gardens. It will enrich your brain, drink it slowly with your meal.

# CHAPTER 16

**The next day** they were taken to another room. Beside the large screen on the wall, each one had a gadget and a television monitor in front of them. "That thing is like a computer, just ask it verbally any question about anything and it will reply you in writing on the screen," Ayond explained.

"Today we will talk about the medallion," Ayond started, "From our archives that little circular thing is a key to activate a device hidden away in a special place in Egypt. It was given to the high priest of the Temple to be given to his son or daughter at the time before his passing. This process should continue indefinitely until such time in the future, someone will come and ask for it. That person has a code word, on saying it, the medallion will respond by blinking a light in its centre. That person would come at any time in the future, so it is important, that the son or daughter entrusted with it must keep it safe. No one outside the family must ever possess or know of it.

"It was meant to activate a device and tell the world about our stay, just in case we are not around in your distant future. But we are still here, and the time has come to tell the world about us, and the contribution we have made to enhance knowledge. In could not be a better time, w*ith what is going on Earth right now, the time is ripe.*

"The priest who was your ancestor," she looked at Sam and Daniel, kept his word. "We lost track of it when his son, who had no children, buried it with him. His act was innocent, he should have retrieved it after he got married later in life, and had children. He must have forgotten all about it. However, thanks to Sam and Daniel we have it now with us. You know the rest of the story.

"Let me tell you, that the Guardian and the Supreme High are pleased with you and have decided to host you as one of us. And, not forgetting David and Jim, because of them you will share the same status and privileges.

"Thank you," murmured David and Jim nodded his heads.

Ayond leaned both hands on the desk, she backed her chair and said looking at Aishtra, "We must leave them alone to play with their computers; leave whenever you wish, and you know the way to your rooms. I will be in touch sometime later."

As soon as they left David spoke with a commanding theatrical voice, and the spreading of his hands, "Well gentlemen you have the floor, any questions?"

At that moment they were interrupted by the arrival of tea and refreshments. They waited for the attendants to leave. They got up almost at once and headed for the tea table.

Jim broke the silence, "I just can't believe what is really happening. Imagine we are sitting in an extra-terrestrial, an alien facility, working with them on some mysterious mission, to announce to the world of their presence, and God knows what they will demand in return."

"I'll tell you what," David interrupted him, "We are now involved in the most enigmatic detective work in history. We may have to travel to Egypt and then," he paused, taking his cup of tea and sandwich to the table, "We have to find some old artefact or some sort of a gadget," he paused, "It just does not make sense to me as to how will it all fit in. Why all the fuss about an old device, why not just do the announcement by a message from the Supreme High, read by the Guardian or Ayond."

"That perhaps will not be as effective as the machine buried thousands of years ago, to prove their claim and presence on our world, much before our current history began," Sam explained.

The rest sat down with their tea and munched on the sandwiches without a word. David cleared his throat with a cough and began, "Then we may have to go to Egypt for sure, and find the device. It is not going to be easy, unless they know where to look. What frightens me, is what it will reveal."

Daniel could not resist but to butt in, "If there is such a gadget, it will not be waiting for us to pick it up. We have to dig for it, but where, and do you think the authorities will allow it? It does not make any sense, unless Ayond knows where it is, and easy to retrieve."

"That makes sense, Ayond may know its location, after all they have it on record in their archives, the Supreme High was there at the time, and surely knows where it was buried, perhaps in one of the Pyramids or the Sphinx, if so, do you think the authorities will allow us dig around," Jim interjected.

"Jim, it makes sense what you have said, and why we are guessing, we were given these computer, perhaps we may find something related to it," Sam said thoughtfully.

They pushed their tea cups aside and began their search. Several minutes passed. Some got up for more tea. The search was on. An hour later someone said, "I give up."

Jim lost his patience, "There are hundreds of Pyramids and no mention of anything found of interest in any, not even the museum says anything about a special relic or gadget found in them."

"Even if they find anything do you think they will publish it? You know very well, in our part of the world they hide all delicate finding from the public, and even lie to cover it up," David put in.

"Now I remember something," Sam added, "It could be the answer. Many years ago I read in a newspapers that some archaeologists were searching in one of the Pyramids for something. A sort of robot machine was used to remove it, but after many tries they failed. They said something about the 'thing', was difficult to reach, and they would bring another machine and try again.

"Were they telling the truth? Did they find something and cover it up. Was it the machine we are looking for? Is it of an alien origin, at that time only they could had built such an object?"

"Well, if we have to go to Egypt, that will be fun and adventure, though risky, but for a noble purpose, worth it," Sam put in.

With those words they decided to call it a day, in their rooms settled on their beds, fully stretched, and were lost in thought.

# CHAPTER 17

**It was late afternoon,** Aishtra called and tunefully asked them to meet in a Sam's room, "We are coming over with some goodies."

Shortly, Ayond and Aishtra walked in with an attendant carrying a tray.

"I have something you have not tasted before. It is gift from the Supreme High, he suggested that as you are part of us, and being very special, you should have this fruit, for that reason he wants you to enjoy its benefits.

"It is a fruit of our world, we grow it here. Looks like your apple, but in the middle of it, there is a syrup. It is as sweet as honey and very addictive, it can induce dreams to virtual reality. In your brain there is a section you haven't used, it is dormant, but will wake up once you eat this fruit. It will give you the ability to project your thoughts in the form of images. For example, if you think of someone, or something, it will materialize in front of you, as a hologram. If it is a living person you can talk to and will reply you back. He or she will communicate with you in his or her dream state or 'think' of you in a wake up state.

"Initially, as it is your first time, you will feel weak and intoxicated. With practice you will have better control. You just taste it for now, chew and swallow very slowly."

They all picket one each, and from their first bite, Ayond noticed the syrup from the fruit flawing through their fingers with them trying to lick it, David and Daniel dropped theirs in the act, Aishtra ran and picked them, "Don't waste them, still good to eat."

Ayond watched with a full grin on her face as they chewed. When they had finished, "You have done well, I will leave you to rest. After your supper, go to sleep. By tomorrow you will feel better. After two days, I will be back with the same fruit, the second application, will begin to take more effect, it will activate and open a box in your brains, which lay dormant, two more after that, you will then feel like a new person, more alert and responsive. In addition, you will be able to heal yourself of ailments." With those words Ayond left.

After she left, all stayed pinned to their seats staring at each other not knowing what to say.

Sam got up and walked to the window, "I need some fresh air."

"We better get back to our rooms, I am already feeling the effect." Daniel said getting up.

The next day all assembled in David's room. "I feel very fresh, no dizziness or the effects of last night," Daniel said pacing the room.

The others expressed the same feeling. "I don't know what is planned for us today. Ayond is perhaps going to change us into super beings," Sam voice was comical.

David was not amused. "I believe in her manipulating our system with good intentions. We have nothing to lose. May be we are being remodelled, using that expression, to be above normal human capabilities." he paused, "Their intentions are good, perhaps a jump forward to our evolutionary state." David stopped when he heard a knock on the door.

Ayond and Aishtra walked in. "Good morning to all, I trust you had a good night's sleep. I can see it on your faces. The juice from the fruit is working on you. Just three more, and you will be experiencing new dimensions. To-day I am going to take you to our library. There we will talk about the medallion."

They left the room with Ayond leading the way. They took an elevator, "Are we moving, can't tell going up or down," Jim looked puzzled.

"Going down, hundred feet or so, the safest area in the facility," Aishtra said to Jim in a whisper.

Seconds later the elevator doors opened. They were greeted by three females, dressed in skin tight fit green clothing, they were beautiful in their twenties.

They led the way through a long corridor with discrete little light along-side the pathway. They stopped in front of a wall. Ayond said something and a screen appeared. She touched it, and again said something, the screen disappeared and a window appeared. A face of a female greeted her and there was a loud click. The wall slid open, and they entered a small room. The door shut behind them and a flood of brilliant light enveloped them. Another door opened and they entered.

They couldn't believe their eyes at the layout, a library with desks lined up in a straight row, on them table lamps, rows of glass cupboards on either side. The lights subdued.

"This is the library gentlemen, you have an unlimited time and access as long as the Grand Master Ayond is with you," one of the girls said.

This was the first time Sam and the rest of the team heard someone addressing Ayond as the Grand Master.

They all turned towards Ayond, looked at her curiously. "It is just a formal address by my staff, the designation of Grand Master makes me the third senior most in the facility. This library can only be excessed by me, it has some of the most treasured books and artefacts.

"Now let's go to the extreme end and take our seats. The three females left the room.

They sat at a round table. Ayond took out the medallion and placed it in front of her. Aishtra laid a large sheet of paper in front of them. On it was a large design of the medallion in black ink.

Ayond flipped the paper and on the back side was the reverse side of it.

"Now you can see clearly what the design is all about. The hand with a key pointing to a door and behind that door is a box. Above the box is a circle with several straight lines, one of the lines on the left is longer almost touching a raised dot. One of the fingers on the hand is also raised. You can feel them, they are protruding. Below the hand and key three separate circles in the middle of each there is a dot. The dots in each circle are not the same. Each one is protruding a little higher than the next.

"On the other side. It is more complicated." Ayond flipped the sheet of paper. "You all look dazed. Didn't you feel the medallion surface when you had it? I suppose it didn't strike you."

Each one of them examined it, running their thumbs in a circular fashion feeling the protrusion, "I wonder what it means," David asked.

"On this side, two hands of a priestess handing over a scroll to a person of authority, and notice the ring that looks like a crown on her finger, on top of which there is what looks like a rectangle or a ruler. The writing inscribed below says, *finally you must understand the truth.*"

Ayond stopped and looked at their bewildered expressions. Some had their mouths open.

"You can read that writing, it is thousands of years old?" Jim asked.

"It is written in our script, it has not changed, and all those symbolic signs are to activate different parts of the device." Ayond explained.

For a long moment no one spoke. It was Daniel who began softly then raising his voice to be heard, "You said it was written in your language, which clearly proves that you have made the medallion, which will activate the gadget or device, and tell the story that you lived on our planet and helped the welfare of the people. When the rest of the world hears your message, they will applause and cheer you."

"I doubt it, there will be those who will feel our presence as an obstacle to their age old thinking, they will surely think it to be a conspiracy to outdo their political and religious beliefs.

Meanwhile Aishtra got up and went to the far end of the room. Minutes later she came with attendants bringing tea and sandwiches.

"During this break, feel free to look around, might spot something interesting," Ayond suggested.

Jim and Daniel got up, walked up to an artefact that stood mounted in a glass casing. "What is it?" Jim asked Ayond who had joined them.

"Can you guess?"

"Looks like a foot print and a pair of shoes next to it."

"Good guess. That is a foot print of the first step made when we landed on Earth and the shoes that made it."

The rest got up and joined them. Minutes later, resumed their session.

Ayond walked up to a cupboard and took out a metal box the size of a thin briefcase. She laid it carefully on the table. She laid her right palm on it, seconds later it clicked open.

With both hands she picked up two metallic sheets and placed them on the table.

"These are drawing of the device we have to find."

The four stood up to have a closer look. "It looks like rectangular box with a lot of markings on it," Jim said looking closer.

"If you look closely, you will see a slot in which the medallion will be inserted with help of another part of the device. A voice will say *'is the world ready to hear the truth'*, of course in our language, I have to press one of these two buttons, 'yes' or 'no'. The box will open and expose a miniature screen like a laptop. I can't tell you more right now until the time is ripe."

"You mentioned another part to be inserted, do you have it?" Sam asked.

"No, but know where it is, I will tell you when we find the main unit," Ayond replied.

Ayond put back the metallic sheets and closed the box. She walked back carrying it carefully to the cupboard.

"Ok gentlemen, enough for today. I will be back this evening with some of the fruit. Again just one each. Have any of you felt a sensation in your eyes, nose and ears. A kind of itching and a double vision at any time?"

Sam promptly replied, "Yes, I did experience a double vision in fact just a few moments ago when I was looking at the foot print and a bit of an itch in my left ear."

"I had an in itch in my eyes and nose last night," Daniel said.

The other two shook their heads in the negative.

Ayond added, "After today's fruit, you will experience more sensations, like dreams related to your forefathers' lives, inherited within your brains. Some humans are lucky to have such dreams naturally, which they innocently associate with remembering a previous life."

On their way out, David commented, "What a library, you must be having books about peoples in other worlds, the history of the universe and how it began."

"Yes we do. Soon, I will arrange that you all may have an excess to this library, and then you can enjoy learning about the vastness of knowledge contained therein.

# CHAPTER 18

**At David's room,** the team sat contemplated at what Ayond had in store for them. To David it was crystal clear. He looked at each of them and with comforting thought he said, "We should be proud to have these people confine in us, and enhancing our physical abilities, the medallion have started it all. They could have taken it and disassociated us, but instead, made us part of them. Sam, and you Daniel, were in centre stage, because of both of you, Jim and I are blessed. Your ancestors worked with the aliens, and now, after nearly two millenniums, we are part of them, search for a lost artefact, when found, will change the world."

They were very attentive to what David has said. No one spoke, waiting to hear more.

"What it will tell us is beyond me. But I can make a guess. It is possible it may indicate a part they played in manipulating our genes. That will not go well.

"Sorry to interrupt you, David," Daniel said, "You know what you are saying. The whole of mankind will be in chaos besides none will believe it. We will be made into a laughing stock and probably be stoned to death."

"Take it easy Daniel. Nobody will pelt us. We will not be the ones to tell the world. They will tell their story, through an official body like the United Nations. It is too early to speculate. Let's find the damned thing first."

Sam got up and walked the bar. "I need a beer, any one," he asked.

They all answered almost simultaneously, "Yes."

"What we have here is not as grave as it looks. What is more serious is the present crisis in the Middle East, and the recent support of some Asian countries, will surely add more fuel to the fire. The waring nations will not listen to any peace maker, they want their pound of flesh." Sam took a sip of his beer and continued.

"I just hope the big powers don't take sides, then will surely escalate to world war III."

Jim came into the conversation by putting a hand onto Sam's shoulder, "Don't be a pessimist my dear friend. In the past we had wars and sooner or later peace was restored."

"In the past there were no weapons of mass destruction, and some crazy guy will use them, and start a chain reaction which will bring death and destruction to both sides." Sam said with a sigh and sat down.

David quaffed his beer and wiped his mouth with the cuff of his sleeve. "What I have to say is that we are living in dangerous time, if we have to go to Egypt to get that thing Ayond is after, we better do it soon. That country is not yet involved, in an instant tempers may flare up, then our venture has to get on hold, until sanity prevails, and that may be after a very long time. If the aliens could show their muscles, perhaps they can drag the waring faction to the table."

"If you remember, Ayond once indicated that they never interfere in Earth matters," Jim recollected.

The conversation continued, until they were exhausted. They sat in silence, when a knock on the door brought them back to their senses. It was Ayond and Aishtra accompanied by an attendant holding a tray with the fruit.

They devoured it mercilessly, licked their fingers not wanting to lose a drop of the juice.

"Tomorrow you will have the final round, two each to speed up the process. The next two days, stay in your rooms, watch television or read, no strenuous activity. On the third day, a doctor will visit and administer a mild fluid into your spine, which is necessary for the fruits to have its full effects. Go to your rooms and relax.

The next two days they were room bound, ate their meals, watched television, read magazines and slept most of the time. Drowsiness and lethargy took hold on the second day, sleep was the only option. On the third day, they woke up fresh and energetic.

The doctor arrived and administered the fluid into the back of the head. "Just relax for an hour after that resume all your normal activities," He advised.

Late afternoon they met at David's room. Chatted casually, at one point Jim got into an argument with Daniel, he was insisting on a mathematical equation that he was right, while Daniel refuted it, and gave his version. Sam and David argued on musical styles.

Ayond and Aishtra arrived, knocked at the door, there was no response, they entered, and stood for a while listening to the heated arguments that were being expounded, with a mischievous tone she joined in.

"You are all wrong, the answer to that equation has never been solved and as far as the musical styles, both composers had different moods at the time they wrote, so both of you are wrong," Ayond burst loud enough for all to soothe down.

"I am impressed, David said looking at Ayond, "You seem to have a good knowledge in both subjects."

Ayond asked them to sit down. "What is happening to you right now, is the latent alignment within your brain, soon it will settle down. You have experienced an urge to get into something that some time in your past, you desired to be, but faded away. It is difficult for you to understand. However, it is a good sign, the fruit has worked well.

"David, what I said about those subjects you were arguing, is all bunkum, just to shut you up. Sorry about that. My visit is to check as to how you are faring, the doctor has given you a clear bill of health as intended to be.

"Shortly an attendant will bring in some special drink, which we shall enjoy together. Moments later it arrived. A tray with six, specially designed glasses, filled to the brim, with greenish fluid.

"Sip it gently, a warmth feeling will ensue, give you an appetite to enjoy the good meal prepared for this occasion. After which, sit for an hour, enjoy the garden outside and go to sleep.

"When you wake up, may have some symptoms of double vision, numbness in the hands, and a mild headache. These can last for a couple of days, stay in your rooms, and wash your face as much as you can, to relieve the drowsiness. On the third day, your physical metabolism would have developed to a more sophisticated level." With those words Ayond and Aishtra left.

That night, each experienced uneasy feelings, woke up several times, splashed water on their faces, twisted and turned in bed, slept with dreams of their childhood, or being in strange unfamiliar locations.

For two days, the discomfort continued, on the following morning, woke up fresh without the anxiety of the previous days. A nurse visited each of them and advised, "Today, just rest, and tomorrow be free to resume your normal activities."

That was perhaps the longest day ever experienced, sitting doing nothing, the magazines had been read and reread, television had nothing new. Sleep was an option, but for how long. No sooner the next day dawned, they were up and about, and gathered in David's room.

After four days of solitary stay confined to their rooms, they had much to talk about, almost without stop the conversation dragged on. After a while, Ayond and Aishtra joined in.

The whole atmosphere turned festive, talking, singing and loud laughter, David explained to Ayond how he had spent the last four days; taking the opportunity of Ayond's undivided attention with David, Sam came close to Aishtra, "I am quite fascinated by you, are you really a Jinn, well your eyes says so, tell me more about your people, do they feelings like us?"

She smiled, "Yes like you, we eat, drink, love, hate and be naughty when we want to tease humans. The only thing we don't have is wars.

"You will be surprised as to how many of us are married to humans. At times when a human male or female refuse us we occupy their bodies, and torture them, it is an irrational act, but when it comes to love, rationality is thrown aside.

"Being a much older civilization, had understood the value of life, in the beginning had gone through thick and thin, but in the end we hit the jack pot. It will be very long before humans could achieve it. Only then, we channelled all our resources to concentrate on technology and medicine.

Our space ships could travel at very high speed using light as a source of energy, could reach the moons of Jupiter or Saturn in days."

"Why those moons?" Sam asked.

"Some of us chose to live there. The solar system is teaming with life, some are very different from you and me."

Sam was amazed by what she was telling him. He thought of the UFO journals he had been reading and the reports of UFO sightings, all seemed to him, must had been the Jinn who darting around and reported as unidentified flying objects. He looked at Ayond and saw her engrossed in conversation with David, Jim and Daniel, he put a direct question to Aishtra, "Can we sometime meet and have dinner privately?"

She agreed, "Of course, we can. Just wait a few more days, after you have fully recovered from the fruit effect, we will have many opportunities." She turned towards Ayond,

"Let's go and join them," She said, and both approached the group.

"Sam, I was just saying, that we are so glad that you all have settled well, and soon, the full impact of the fruit you have eaten, will bracket your abilities almost like ours. I think we had enough for today, rest as much as possible. Drink plenty of water.

"In your present condition, you will experience many dreams, of your childhood, parents and loved ones, even places you had never visited, but are recollections from inherited ancestral memories. Simply explained as accumulated genetic memories."

No sooner, the door closed behind them they all spoke simultaneously. They talked about the effect of the fruit and Daniel said with a smile, "It is like the fruit of wisdom Eve ate."

"I liked the bit when she said accumulated genetic memories, perhaps will see some interesting images of the secret lives my ancestors may have had. My brain will 'remember' and I will watch!" David philosophised.

"Well, we'll know by tomorrow," Jim casually put in.

"Let's look at it in a positive way," Sam had another view point, "We are being physically prepared, not to go Egypt, but perhaps for something much greater, and for what, I can't even make a guess. Whatever it might be, we are in good hand, alien hands!"

Daniel threw up his hands, "I can't think straight any more. I am a servant of the church, suddenly I have become a scientist and a philosopher, and the two do not go very well with what I have been trained for." He paused for a while, all were attentive, waiting for his next utterance, crossed himself, looked up, and said softly, "Forgive me, for I have sinned, *but I like it.*"

All looked at him with reverential awe, and Sam with a mischievous smile and sarcasm hailed, "Well said."

"Sam, I meant what I said, come to think of it, knowledge in any form is good, we must lift the hood from our eyes and be with the real world or better still, *the truth.*" Daniel said softly.

# CHAPTER 19

David woke up half drowsy yawned several times and tried to get out of bed, sat up and the room seemed to spin around him, fell back and shut his eyes. Soon he was asleep, breathing heavily.

Jim had the same experience as David.

Sam managed to struggle out of bed, went to the wash room, splashed water on his head and face. Drank some water and went back to bed.

Daniel had the least effect. He looked in the mirror, his face was flushed and slightly swollen. Decided to sleep it off.

By late afternoon, they woke up, with all the morning effect had gone. Soon they met at David's room.

"What a night, felt like floating, it is all over now," Jim comforted himself and added, "I hope so."

They lazed around, Sam shouted, I am famished, how about ordering lunch?"

David made the order.

After lunch, Jim stood in front of the door, looked into the garden and stretched in full, "I feel the new me," He said.

"You spoke too soon," Daniel interrupted, "Suddenly I am seeing some flashes in my eyes, now I see my church, it is so clear like watching it on a screen. There are some people outside the gate talking to the priest. The scene changed, it is a face I don't recognize. He is dressed in medieval cloths. The vision has gone."

"Ring up your man and ask him if there were people gathered outside the church." Sam suggested.

Daniel called the cell number of the priest. He confirmed what Daniel saw, "And there was a homeless guy in shattered clothing, begging for food." The priest said to Daniel.

"Gentlemen, I am seeing things too," Jim said rubbing his eyes, "I am seeing my wife hanging her laundry. Now I see a farm house, and children playing in the field."

Moments later both David and Sam began to experience visions. The all sat down and shut their eyes. No one spoke for a long while. David dosed off and began to snore. The others just looked at him as he lay.

Sam put his mouth to his ears wanted to wake him up, "Don't do that," Jim said, "He is in a state of semi unconsciousness, waking him up may cause mental glitch, let's take it easy and relax.

Just then Sam, rubbing his eyes, "I am seeing flashes of lights, large orange coloured dot, it's changing its texture to what looks like craters on the moon, and next to it a large statue and a building.

The face on the statue is of a women. It's gone, feeling dizzy, better have a shut eye, why don't we all stretch a bit, it might help." Sam lay beside David.

Daniel and Jim put their legs on to the table and shut their eyes.

An hour later there was a knock on the door, not receiving a respond, Ayond entered. Daniel heard the knock took his time, he was halfway and greeted her with a big yawn.

She entered to a scene of lifeless bodies strewn on the bed and chairs.

"I will wake them up. We all had a dizzy spells and couldn't keep our eye open. We have been seeing images."

Ayond was amused, she sat and shifting her head from left to right. Looking at the lifeless bodies. She walked up to Sam, touched him gently and woke him up. Daniel managed to wake up rest.

Soon they were all up and about, yawned as they talked, it became contagious, even Ayond yawned a couple times.

To remedy the situation, Ayond made a call.

An attendant brought in a tray with seaming hot purple liquid in thin long glasses.

"Be careful, the glasses are cold from the outside, but the drink is hot, just sip it slowly." She advised.

Daniel was the last to finish, with a loud smack of the tongue, "That was delicious, can I have another one," He said putting the glass down.

"Sorry Daniel, one is sufficient, go and slash some water on you faces, have to leave for some therapy, just a routine. A scan test, spend a few minutes under a column of light. That will strengthen your muscles and other faculties. Once done, your internal organs like, heart, kidneys, and liver will have an added strength and adapt to your new mental enhancement.

The therapy lasted an hour, after which they were told, there will be one more, of a different type after a few days.

When they got into the vehicle, Ayond exclaimed, "Now we go and have some fun." Aishtra was at the wheel. They arrived at gate, entered and all got off. Ayond led them through a narrow passage and stopped at a brassy door. She place her left palm on it and slid opened. The room they entered was dark, but to their surprise, when their eyes became accommodated, hundreds of pin light dotted the ceiling, David exclaimed, "What a view, reminds me of a planetarium."

"More than that, please follow me." They gathered under a beam of crimson coloured light, "Look up, I will chose a star from up there and go visit it. Yes, I literally meant what I said, see people, and walk on their roads.

"David hold my hand firmly, and you hold that of the person next to you, and so on until we are all connected. Don't leave them until I say so. On a remote in her free hand, she punched on it using her thumb. The column of light began to change colours and rotate.

"I am beginning to feel as if I am rotating with the lights," Sam said excitedly.

"Yes you are, just remain still, it will take you up there," Ayond said.

Suddenly the lights went out. They felt as left floating in the void of space.

"We are floating, and can see a light approaching, it is getting brighter, and too strong to look at it, must be a sun." One of them said.

"No, not a sun but the reflected light from a planet," Aishtra voiced.

They approached a cloud formation, flew through it, almost feeling its fluffy touch, rubbing against their faces.

A city appeared below them, with flying vehicles, the size of a car, darted all over. Finally they felt their feet touch the ground.

"Now you can leave your hands free, we are in a park, see those people playing with children, go and meet them," Ayond suggested.

David walked up, and greeted them in English. There was no reaction, Jim shouted, "They don't understand our language, just wave your hands."

Still no response, he walked up to one of the men and put his hands on his shoulder, David's hand went through him and quickly pulled back.

"What the," he did not finish his sentence, when he heard Ayond behind him, "They can't see or feel you. You are in astral travel. An out of body experience. It is artificially induced by our machines. The monks in Tibet have achieved this ability by concentration and meditation."

"Those people are just like us, which planet is this?" David asked.

"Just a planet in the Milky Way, we have details of it in our library, go and enjoy a walk in the Park."

Sam and Jim strolled and talked endlessly. Daniels stayed with Ayond and Aishtra.

Soon they gathered around Ayond and held hands, she pressed on to something on the remote, and a hallo began to form, surrounding them. The same process was repeated in reverse, back to the point where they started.

"That was an experience, like a dream, where you experience such a phenomena only in your sleep," Daniel said.

"That brief adventure was to illustrate what you can do, with a bit of meditation and concentration, in time you can achieve what you have experienced without the aid of that machine, on your own." Ayond said as the moved out.

"It is a form of relaxation or meditation when you are alone, to be in the timeless void, travel to places at will and enjoy the beauty of nature. Use it wisely, it a great gift you will ultimately muster," Ayond said and led them out of the planetarium.

Aishtra drove through meandering tunnels and reached a building with Roman style carved pillars.

Inside there were statues of Cicero, Plato, Socrates, Archimedes, Pythagoras, and a host of Earthy figures including Abraham Lincoln and Elbert Einstein.

"What is this place? Jim asked.

"From the outside, looks like a museum, but inside, is one of our most sophisticated physical therapy to reinforce what you had gone through earlier. Once over, your bodies would endure any strains or stresses as our people are capable of.

"Listen to me carefully, while going through the process, obey all instruction to the letter. The operators are not made of flesh and blood, but machines. A nurse will be there to guide and stand bye in case of an accident, any false move could cost you a limb or your life. I will not be there, only when completed they will bring you to me. Any questions?"

"Just one," Sam replied nervously, "Is it a must we have to go through with this."

"Yes Sam, it is a must for your own good. After having taken the fruit, the brain and body began to respond to the changes taking place within the system, and this operation will make it durable as long as you live. In simple English, you will become immune to any disease and self-healing in case of injury. Your brain power will keep developing many folds. So please do this exercise diligently and listen to your nurse, the whole operation will take about thirty minutes. By the way, this entire operation was recommended by the Supreme High, he has his reasons."

While Ayond was talking to Sam, four female walked up, dressed in grey skin tight outfits, Their head covered with what looked like a facial mask, eyes large and shiny, almond shaped. "Don't let their eyes worry you, they are wearing a sort of dark glasses, to cover their eyes from the laser beams."

One by one they left with their escorts. In a room they were undressed and made to wear similar attire as their escorts. Ayond

137

and Aishtra moved to another section in the building. The Guardian was in there sitting in front of a screen.

"The Supreme High had asked me to join you, we can all see the operation together. Right now, they are being strapped to the machines," the Guardian said softly.

The scene moved from one bed to the other as the machines came to life and began its function. Strapped on to their beds, with legs wide apart and their heads connected to numerous wires leading to a glass globe, the subjects lay firmly pinned. Watched attentively, each receiving a doze of intricate movements of robotic hands beaming its ray on to the subjects.

The four in attendance were standing beside each of them, with an instrument in their hand.

"The instrument they are holding can stop the machine instantly, only if there is a malfunction but not soon enough to prevent any harm. Remember what had happened to our previous initiates some time ago. They fooled us but not this machine, it read their devious minds to abuse this gift for their personal ends. Pity they were vaporized," the Guardian said, and continued, "Once this is over, must think of obtaining that box from Egypt. The situation in the Middle East in becoming more explosive day by day. Must get it, to tell the world how to behave. It can bring them to their senses, or turn them more violent.

"I am seeing blinking light around their beds, it is a signal that it is coming to an end."

They were interrupted by voice saying, three subjects had successfully qualified, one, Mr. Daniel needs urgent treatment to his skin, must take him to an incubator. The procedure will take one hour. May I have your permission to perform?"

The Guardian instructed to proceed.

"Coming back to what we were talking about, doubtful to predict, though I tend to agree on the latter, some may refuse to see logic, still live in the days of medieval ignorance. Many nations on their pay role, will support them blindly.

"Some of the super powers and most of the western nations would accept the message in good fate, but some, would remain silent, which would encourage the trouble makers.

"You know how some powers are, have double standard; support, reject or look the other way." The Guardian concluded.

Ayond looked at him, "It is those with money or resources corrupt nations and can influence a decision, good or bad." Ayond observed.

The Guardian paced the room and stood in front of a globe of the world at one corner of the room, touched it and added, "Only a New World Order would be an answer, and implement it rigidly for its success.

"The virus reported in south Asia is another threat, has spread fast to the east as far as North Korea. At this rate, soon this epidemic, will spread to the Middle East and Europe. We have obtained a sample, under very strict quarantine conditions, the Supreme High is analysing it.

A voice through a speaker announced, "We have completed the treatment of Mr Daniel, two days of rest is recommended."

"Excellent, our team is able and ready, we should allow them a vacation rest period for a few days." Ayond was delighted.

Turning to the Guardian, "The virus situation is alarming, could get out of hand and bring about a global catastrophe if not checked in time."

"The newspapers estimate that over three million dead since it started four months ago, and have no clue how and what caused it," The Guardian added.

"We had the plague in Europe, some hundreds years ago, took the lives of millions, but they got the root cause of it, with today's technology should be able to squash this culprit. Perhaps, it is a natural phenomenon to check population growth, a situation arises every so many hundreds or thousands or even a million years, and even could be a process of evolutionary jump start to get rid of the old replacing with something better, one example was the eradication of the dinosaurs, though it was a different catastrophe, but we had a near to total eradication of life due to climatic conditions. I am just theorising, it may mean nothing." Ayond was carried away.

"Well, back to our present immediate requirements." The Guardian was serious. "Go to Egypt and get that box or device, which they have retrieved from the Pyramid, and by the way, there is another part which was hidden separately in the vicinity. Easy to get to. You know where it is. The Supreme High and I were there then when we put them, and now we are still here, how lucky we are not to be human."

"Our team must be bored waiting," Ayond said, went out and brought then in.

"Congratulations everybody, you are now as good as we are.' She exclaimed and hugged each one of them. The Guardian hugged the four with one embrace, surrounded within his arms.

# CHAPTER 20

**Early evening,** the next day, young female attendants filed in carrying trays of food, each one, a stunning beauty. While they ate, Sam and his companions were experiencing a treat they could never have imagined. The attendants gently massaged their shoulders and backs, occasionally helped them with placing morsels of food in their mouth. Wine flowed, when a glass emptied, replacement came promptly, music played, low-key lighting added to the noir ambiance; the atmosphere was like page from the Arabian Nights!

The only thing Sam could remember the next morning was one of the beautiful attendants sleeping next to him. He got out of bed and stood admiring the figure that lay beside him minutes before. "That is what I call a perfect creation." He muttered and went for a shower. She got up and slipped away, when he returned, to his disappointment she was gone.

They gathered at David's room and each had a story to tell. Daniel was first to speak. "I felt like a new person, I could not help but to let the animal in me take over."

Sam interrupted him, "Daniel, after all you are human like all of us, the charade you have been living in, has vanished, the true you has emerged, if you know what I mean."

David added, "We are men my league, nothing to complain about, it was perhaps the initiation that prompted us to indulge into supressed and latent desires. We still have another day to relax, let's make the best of it, come what may. I love to be here, and proud to be associated in their venture to find a missing artefact."

Breakfast, lunch and afternoon tea was served without an incident. Sam, fiddled around with an equipment and chose Brahms's symphony No.1 and allowed it to fill the room at full blast. They sat quietly and listened, when it finished they lay still, some had their eyes closed and someone shouted, "Play it again, Sam!"

When it was over, Jim suggested to go out into the garden for some fresh air. They all joined him. "What a place, the trees, the birds chirping and the aroma from the flowers reminds me of the outside world. They have done this place too well to be below the surface. It must have taken them years to build it."

"Don't worry your head with it, right now let's enjoy its pleasures," David put in.

They lazed around and spent their time in general gossip. Dinner time was approaching and they decided to go inside. To their surprise, eight females greeted them with one voice, "Welcome gentlemen, your dinner is ready." The same greeting gestures as the night before.

A table lay in the middle of the room with a variety of dishes. Two attendants busied at the little bar pouring wine.

The four stood stunned, and were dazed by their beauty, Sam commented, "They are fit to pose in a beauty contest, not to be serving us."

"I am hungry, let's not stand to formalities," David was the first to help himself. Followed by Jim and Sam. Daniel went to one of the females and politely asked, "What's all this in honour of. Is there a special occasion we are celebrating, again?"

"We are celebrating your success, just eat and drink and be merry. We are here to help you achieve that," she replied with a musical tone.

Daniel was mesmerised by her reply, and headed to the dining table.

David and Sam exchanged glances, unsure of how to react, the night before was in the past, should they indulge or abstain. But soon, the flirtatious service began, wine glasses brought to their lips while they feasted, the music loud and soon dancing began.

However, as time went by, they settled down and began exchanging jokes, to which Jim excelled, causing loud burst of laughter. The females out-numbered the men, it was not a problem, Daniel and Jim had two on either side and their moods were explosive.

The party went on for hours, five attendants began to clear the table and left. Three remained, each talking to David, Jim and Daniel, Sam was left alone, he discretely left the room and went outside into the garden. He noticed a figure sitting on a chair under a tree. He curiously walked towards it. To his surprise it was Aishtra, "What are you doing here?" He asked with an element of surprise and joy in his voice.

"Came to see you, it is my time off and want to spend it with you."

"What if Ayond sees you, what will she say?"

"Nothing, in fact she suggested if I wish to spend some time with you."

"Great, I love to, come on lets go to the other side of the garden, we'll have some peace from the noisy lot."

They walked gently and Sam felt her hand lock into his. "How did you get in here, we did not see you come in?"

"Remember I am Jinn, can go where I please, without being seen. I can appear and disappear at will."

They exchanged a few sentences when they heard a voice calling for Sam. It was Daniel, walking about the garden. Before he could see them they walked up to him.

"Don't make such a commotion," Sam introduced Aishtra and added, "You met Aishtra before."

Daniel with mouth open, "How, and where did she come from?"

"Never mind that, what have you come for?"

"We thought you were alone, worried about you."

"I am in good hands," suddenly they were interrupted by David, Jim and their female partners.

The party have moved to the garden. Sam didn't like it, but had to comply. They chatted, sang and danced until they were exhausted.

They dispersed to their room with their partners and Sam with Aishtra.

Sam and Aishtra sat together on a stretched sofa with a reclining back-rest, "I could not believe my eyes when I saw you in the garden, now we are together let me introduce myself, more properly," Sam began but Aishtra put hand to his mouth, "I know everything about you. Who is your father and how you are related to Michael and Daniel. You come from a long line going back to the time your ancestor was a senior priest in an Egyptian temple in the first century BCE. Your ancestors encounter with extra-terrestrial beings and you know the rest."

"So you all have a detail records of our family. How come and why? He interrupted.

"You had the medallion we have been looking for, besides that your ancestor worked with us."

"OK, how about telling me something about yourself."

"You are forgetting, I had explained my story to all of you."

"Yes you did, how about telling something about your life style as a Jinn. Something more personal, how the Jinn live, their family system, and you mentioned that you have marriages with humans."

"Jinn are a civilised society. Of course we have good guys and bad guys, just like you humans, and a few very notorious bad ones who conspire with equally bad humans and teach them the so called magic. Yes, some of our men and women have fallen in love with human, some end in marriage but most just have a romance.

"Because of our physical structure we can appear and disappear at will. Travel long distance in seconds even in space we don't need oxygen. Remember we are made of electromagnetic energy or smokeless fire as you humans call us. Enough talk, I am feeling tired after a long day."

Sam moved closer and put his arms around her. He came close to her face and kissed her. She reciprocated and they were in a long embrace.

Moments later they retired to the bedroom, removed her clothes as she walked. Sam did the same and both jumped on to the bed, they were locked in an embrace and kissed endlessly.

Aishtra's body began to light up, Sam felt the heat of her body as it began to emit more light, for an instant he uttered a moan as his body began to light up too. The light from both became so intense that their physical shape infused to became one blob of intense glow. It lasted for several minutes.

They separated and Sam fell on his back almost gasping for breath. The lights vanished, she put her arm across his chest and said to him in a whisper, "Good night Sam, have nice dreams."

When he woke up in the morning she was gone. He sat up in bed, looked at the watch, "Too early," he said to himself and went back to sleep.

It was about ten in the morning David called, asked him to be ready and meet at noon.

When they met no one said anything about the night before. David broke the silence, "Ayond called, she will take us to the briefing room at 1600 hours." He looked at Daniel, "You look tired, haven't had sufficient sleep?"

Daniel replied sheepishly, "Oh! Yes a good sleep, just kept chatting till late at night."

"Chatting or something else," Sam said sarcastically.

David looked at Sam disapprovingly, "Leave him alone, we all had long chats too."

Breakfast was served and they had the tea in the garden. Jim suggested that they request Ayond to go out and visit their homes for a day or two. It was agreed that Sam should put the question to her.

"We'll ask her after our meeting this evening."

# CHAPTER 21

**It was nearly 1600 hours** and Jim was the first to jump up from his reclining position and rushed to the wash room, "Ayond should be here at any moment, better freshen up."

Daniel got up lazily still groggy from his slumber. Sam and David straighten themselves and headed for the mirror. Minutes later all were presentably prim and proper to meet with their hostess.

David slid the door open and waited with two bouquets of flowers which he had plucked from the garden. He presented them to Ayond and Aishtra as they came in.

"This is from all of us to thank you for your excellent hospitality."

"Thank you all for your kind gesture." Ayond said appreciably. She walked in and sat down, Aishtra dragged a chair and sat beside her. Why don't you all sit down and listen carefully what I am going say to you. Aishtra stole a glimpse at Sam and gave him a gentle smile. Sam was already staring at her and he reciprocated.

Ayond began, "Gentlemen, today as I am speaking right now, you have perfected your mental and physical abilities and have become one of us. You have passed all tests, though human, you are far above the level of your species.

"The task ahead of us is not easy, it will take some courage to accomplish."

Jim was thinking as to when to pop up his request to go and visit his wife. "Perhaps after the meeting, if Sam forgets to ask."

Ayond continued, "We are going to another section of the facility, where you will be given an ID code printed on to you palm, not visible to the eye, With that you are free to excess all parts of the facility accept the special zone where the Supreme High resides."

They got into a vehicle and off they went. They crossed a long bridge below which they could see little houses and cattle grazing like any country side scene. "How big is this place," Sam asked.

"Very big and it is all underground. The light is artificial, all was made many years ago," Aishtra replied.

"Does anybody else know of this place," Sam looked at Ayond for a reply.

"Just a handful, a special department in the government only knows of our presence, not even the Prime Minister knows of our existence. We have the freedom to do as we please."

The vehicle slowed down and took a turn and stopped in front of a large glass door. They entered the building and Ayond led them to a metallic sliding door which she opened by placing her palm on a panel.

The room was dimly lit, it had long tables stretching the length of the room with chairs on either side. The walls were decorated with classical earthly artworks. Ayond sat at the head of the table with Aishtra at her right side.

Two males dressed in tight fit grey attire, one holding an instrument and the other some shining metallic sheets the size of a palm.

Ayond requested each of them to put their right hand forward and press on to the sheet, as they did, there a buzz from the machine. On the metallic sheet, their hand impressions feature clearly. When all was done, Ayond thanked the two men and they left.

"These sheets will be given to the special department of your government for your safety in your part of the world whenever you are outside. Now let's get into business."

A large screen on the wall came to life. "Coming to the medallion you have found, you know of our association with the ancestors of Sam Daniel and Michael, we also had many humans working with us, but you three are special because your ancestor was entrusted with something that will tell the world who we are and our contributions to mankind.

"Humans are good learners, but some have abused the knowledge given, for selfish ends.

"For now let's concentrate on the medallion. There are two items to be found, one is laying, hidden away in the museum in Cairo, after being found. The other is within the Sphinx, and I know where it is. Once both items are with us, we will be able to activate the device by the insertion of the medallion.

"We will consult with some governments or perhaps through the United Nations, and read out the message put many years ago for the benefit of future generations. There would be those who would not appreciate our gesture, and may create confusion, turmoil and social unrest, which would be the catalyst for another enemy of mankind to surface and join hands with the trouble makers."

Jim shuffled in his chair and put up a hand, "Forgive me to interrupt, what other enemy,"

"I am coming to that Jim, it is unbelievable but true. When we came to this planet about fifteen and half thousand ago, we found a race of people not of this planet. They were an aliens from another world. They were interested in mining gold and salt mostly in South Africa and India. They were selfish, used people as slaves, we had to get rid of them. We fought a war, destroyed all their equipment and left only their mother ship to take them back where they came from. They were told never to return. Most likely they are living somewhere in the solar system, watching for an opportunity to return, as long as we are here, Earth is safe." After a short pause she continued, "With that enemy gone, we were free to settle down, not as masters but as equals. The rest of the story you have been told. To refresh your memory, we built monuments all over the world, some to act as beacons for our ships and some fancy structures like the Pyramid in Africa and the Americas and in some other locations.

"Seeing our flying ships and ability to haul massive rocks, they treated us as gods, we tried to convince them otherwise, but to no avail.

"To cut the long story short, the idea to build the Sphinx came when flying over the Carpathian Mountains in the country you call Romania, saw a head of a man, carved naturally on a mountain top, liked the concept, decided to build one with the head of a tribal leader of the time, to honour him. I am tired of repeating this story, however some other time perhaps, I must go, have an urgent business to attend to, go and relax, Aishtra can stay, to enlighten you more on what we have talked today."

"Good idea," Sam said with a wink to Aishtra.

They opted to continue at David's room.

Jim and Daniel sat down with their feet resting on the tables while Sam opened the door to the garden and stepped out with Aishtra, David threw himself on to the bed.

Sam and Aishtra sat under a tree where no one could disturb them. They embraced and cuddled. Time went by. Sam suggested they move to his room, "You go and will join you later," Aishtra suggested and left.

Sam looked at David and covered him with a blanket, closed the garden door and did his best to put the room in a presentable condition.

He entered his room, brushed his teeth, and changed into his pyjamas. His eyes caught a glimpse of some movement in his bed. He pulled the sheet and, "Surprise!" Aishtra screamed putting both her hand in a greeting gesture. Sam stared at her naked body and for a moment stood amazed then flung himself on to her.

With all what went on during the day, Sam and Jim forgot to ask Ayond for a furlough to go and meet family and friends.

# CHAPTER 22

Sam woke up early, Aishtra was gone, and soon he joined the others in David's room. They breakfasted almost in silence. The news on the TV was alarming. Syria and Lebanon were exchanging border fire with Israel. It said, Syrian aircrafts were shot down and Israeli tanks have entered into Lebanon. The situation was tense, none of the sides listened to the UN's call to halt the war.

Ayond came rushing and suggested they meet the Guardian immediately. Not knowing what the urgency was, they got into a vehicle with Aishtra at the wheel.

In the room with a raised pedestal and seven chairs they sat, leaving one in between Ayond and Aishtra for the Guardian. He walked in with two persons and they were talking. He waved a hand at Ayond and the rest and continued to talk to the two men, after they left, walked up the pedestal, "Sorry for keeping you waiting, I had to give those two final instructions to go to Egypt and prepare for your arrival there."

"The situation in the Middle East is tense and may escalate into a crazy war, I hope the UN and the major powers can bring a cease fire, and be neutral in the present circumstances. We are most unhappy with some of the western nations. It is believed that some of them had fuelled this madness. Another major problem, surfaced in China, and Eastern Europe. I don't think Ayond mentioned it to you."

He explained that a virus had spread from south Asia into China, Mongolia and beyond. From India up north into Afghanistan and creeping northwards, soon will hit southern Russia and Europe.

"Unstoppable, the use of some chemicals, instead of eradicating it, boosted its growth to an ant size bug. The Supreme High has no solution. People are dying by the millions, nature has declared a war.

"Before it gets to Africa, we must act fast to obtain those devises in Egypt at any cost. You all will leave next week, the two gentlemen who were with me earlier, will be there to meet you at the airport. They are highly qualified, know that country well, should you face any trouble, they are there to help."

Looked at Aishtra, "Besides, you have the capable hands of Aishtra, being a Jinn, can do wonders. I will meet you again before your departure, in the meanwhile you can go to your homes, meet loved ones, for a day or two. Avoid talking about your trip or what you do, secrecy of your mission is imperative."

With that he got up and shook hands with all. "Ayond bring me those items, you know where to look."

At their living quarters, Ayond further briefed them about what to expect in Egypt, "They are friendly people, millions of tourist visit it, but we are no tourists, going to take back what belongs to us, of course they don't know it, use any means, short of stealing." She paused, to let what she said sink in.

"The trick is to act as innocent tourists, flash the colour of money generously, not to get too friendly or intimate with authorities, they can be nasty, if there is a hint or suspicion of what we are after, can lead to imprisonment or death.

"Show keen interest in Egyptian history, even to extent that we are gathering information for a document, and important of all, act very normal.

"As for your visits to your families, a car will take you tomorrow, and tell the driver when and where to pick you up.

# CHAPTER 23

**The next day,** after breakfast they left. He driver was told to drop David first, it was a refreshing drive, after so many days living indoors. On reaching his home, David got off and waved, "See you in a couple of days gentlemen."

He settled at his desk and let his thought wander about the events that led him into a new perspective, away from his former routine existence. "I thank Sam for that, that little piece of metal, the medallion, started it all, and where will we land up at the end." With those recollections, he dozed off on the chair.

Next was Jim, no sooner he got off the car, his wife gave him a nasty reception. "Who do think you are, leaving us high and dry, and closing the shop, I hope it is not a woman you are after."

"Too old for that," Jim put his hands around her and gave her a kiss. "I got a very special assignment to help a friend in need," he was thinking fast as to what will pacify her, "This friend had a serious problem with his only son who has been accused of disturbing the peace and thrown into prison and,"

She cut in, "I don't care what he did, you are always helping people and in return no one helps you."

He was comfortable, "She fell for it," he said to himself.

"What is it you said," she turned and faced him.

"Nothing dear, I am dying for a cup of tea."

He decided to tell her, that he has to go away for some time, but how. When she had cooled down, he casually said, "I have to go to France as that boy is there," Before he could finish, she interrupted. "Our two boys are there, look them up before you return."

He was delighted, "She fell for it."

Daniel was too glad to see that all was in good order in the church.

He explained that he is working on a project that will benefit the church and mankind, and he has to be away for some time.

The caretaker priest just replied, "Anything good for the church, good for me, carry on what you are doing. I am beginning to like this place. Getting to know the parish, and planning to have a little festival next week, "Wish you are here to join us."

"Perhaps on my return we will have another one, you will have to excuse me this time."

Sam found the house empty, no sign of Michael. He decided to sleep.

He woke up with jump as Michael stormed into the room with a loud welcoming greetings.

Sam briefed him of what had happened the weeks he was away but avoided mentioning the Guardian and the Supreme High. He thought it perhaps too early to talk about them. Too farfetched for him to understand the situation. But he briefly mentioned that he has to travel.

Michael was not too attentive to what Sam was narrating to him.

"Do what you have to do, so long as you don't get in trouble and bring shame to our ancestral home. Just tell me the bottom line when you find what we are looking for." Michael casually said.

Michael reiterated, "You know me well, and want to know more, but don't involve me. I am a respected government servant with a reputation, don't want people to start rumours and what not."

He was least interested, a matter of fact person. Dedicated government servant and had no time for adventure. To Sam, it was clear that Michael will not stand in his the way, and was free to do as he pleased, especially with the artefacts down there in his house.

That evening they went to a small Tavern in the village. They talked about the room where N is buried. Both agreed to seal the room permanently, "Use several coats of paint, to last for a very long time, as far as the documents and artefacts, display them nicely on a table, for anyone to look at." Michael recommended.

The next day Sam was in full swing. He got the bricks and all what was needed, stacked them in the little space down below, stood for some time and looked into the room, touched the stone slab covering N's tomb, adjusted the contamination suit on to the chair, and with full zeal and zest, began laying the bricks to seal the entrance to the room that held a secret for nearly two centuries. The paint job was not easy, first he had to do up the wall and the bricked doorway with plaster, and by late evening finished the paint work. He sat and admired his expertise.

Without wasting time, started the finishing touches to the stone door that would only open from the inside, just as Michael wanted.

When Michael arrived, he took him down, "I can't believe that you did all this in one day. Glad that our secret shall remain buried behind that wall, and how beautiful that stone door looks," Walked up, to test it, flung it open. Walked up the adjacent room that was stacked with unwanted materials, had on a table neatly arranged and well displayed family heir looms.

He was emotionally moved, and warmly embraced Sam, "I am going to miss you, and I have a feeling that we may not see each other in a long time. Wherever you go, remember, you have a home to come to."

# CHAPTER 24

**At 10 in the morning** David stood outside his gate and waited for the transport to take him back to the facility. He sat in the front seat and wished the driver, "Good morning, it is a nice sunny day."

The driver replied, "Yes sir, it is." That was the only conversation until they reached Jim's place.

He was nowhere to be seen. They waited patiently, Jim appeared with his wife talking loud and without stopping. He turned to her, "Honey don't worry, I will be all right. It is just a few days. I will be back without you realizing it. He kissed her and got into car waving out of the window as they sped away.

Daniel was waiting outside the church alone. He wished the occupants in the car as he settled in, "Pleasant day, have you guys had a good time? I had a pleasant two days."

David and Jim murmured something and no one spoke after that. The final pick up was Sam. Saw Michael standing with Sam hugging each other as the car halted beside them. Sam got into the car and Michael wished them a pleasant and successful journey with hands waving.

At the facility, they freshened up and met at David's room. Shortly, there was a knock at the door. Aishtra came to collect them to meet with the Guardian.

"Hope you had an enjoyable trip with you families. Regarding your trip to Egypt, take all precautions to stay out of trouble, the two men I have sent will keep an eye on you. Once you have the two devises, must leave immediately, and you Aishtra carry them by your means of travel, and bring them to me."

Then the Guardian brought up the virus situation. "It is spreading fast, from its microbial status, developed into a bug, and recently it was reported, grown further to the size of beetle. What makes it grow, we have no idea and is multiplying fast.

"The Supreme High with all his wisdom has no answer. We'll keep you posted of further development. Africa is safe, no reports so far. I will leave you now and wish you a successful trip," he waived a hand and left.

Ayond had some pamphlets and sheets of paper to distribute. "This little booklet tells you all about the Pyramids and the Sphinx. It is published by the Egyptian authorities, a straightforward information, on a sheet of paper is our travel plans. I have left the return journey open, depending on when we finish our task. Our two men there, will handle the return trip.

"We leave here tomorrow late afternoon. Our flight is at eight in the evening, we shall be in Cairo by about seven the following morning."

Back in David's room, they chatted about their trip. "I have seen pictures and videos, but now I can touch them and meet with the Pharaoh's mummy." Jim was talking to the pamphlet.

The next morning they waited for Ayond to show up, no sooner she arrived, headed for the waiting stretched limousine, though they were cramped inside, they adjusted well.

The flight took off on time and the announcement said they should reach Cairo at seven thirty in the morning.

At Cairo airport, standing in the immigration queue, Ayond turned to Sam standing behind her, "My last visit was in the fifties. Cairo has changed. It was not as crowded as it is now."

The two men sent by the Guardian were there to meet them.

They sailed through immigration in minutes, British passports needed no visa. As soon as they stepped out of the airport, chaotic coolie handlers rushed to help with their luggage. Both men, pushed them aside and picked three. Taxi drivers demanded two hundred Egyptian Pounds each for the trip to the Hilton Hotel. Seeing they were European, the price was boosted up. The men familiar with local bargaining, offered each seventy pounds, and turned away to look for another, promptly the drivers agreed on eighty pounds.

At the hotel, porters unloaded their luggage, and after checking in at the reception desk, they went to their rooms which were next to each other. The porters place the suit cases in each room and surrounded them with extended hands. This time, Sam took out his wallet and paid them generously.

"I have chosen this hotel because it is opposite the Cairo Museum. We have just to walk across," Ayond said as she settled down on the sofa.

"You all freshen up and will meet in my room in about two hours, it is a bit early, and the museum opens at 10:30 according to the pamphlet."

Going to the museum was an ordeal, though it was a short distance from the hotel, they had to meander through a flood of pedestrians, avoid vehicles of all sizes blowing their horns ceaselessly from running them over, and to top it all the slow but rash animal carts, at one time Jim brushed his head with a donkey that almost ran him over. Finally arrived at the steps of the Museum. Climbed up and stood next to statue. Looked back at the square they had just crossed, the car horns were deafening.

Inside the museum roamed freely, decided to split up and meet an hour later at the entrance gate.

Besides genuinely inspecting each items, they kept their eyes open for any indication to what they were looking for. To them it was obvious, such an antique and enigmatic artefact would not be on display.

They repeated the drill to visit the museum three days in a row, the same routine, and stop at an object, make notes, look fascinated, and spend time at a mummy, as in communication with the dead. Their acts were meticulously performed.

All this has not gone to waste, but helped to get the attention of a young employee, who perhaps is in the habit to lure innocent tourist with fancy talk to make a few pound on the side. And, that was exactly what Ayond was fishing for.

He made his move, on the fifth day as the gathered outside the museum to leave, "Hello ladies and gentlemen, you seem to like our museum, I can explain more in details than what you read in our pamphlets. We have many thing ordinary people don't understand." He spoke good English but with a strong Arabic accent.

Ayond studied him, "Perhaps, he can deliver more than what he says," Was her immediate thought.

"Yes, it is very rich, it will take us weeks to see it all," Ayond put in nicely to the man.

"I can help you to understand better if you hire me," he offered candidly.

Ayond probably had found the person, who may start the ball to roll, in her favour.

She wanted to capitalise on her finding, but did not want to show it, with a low key, she replied him, "Actually we don't need a guide we know quite a bit about mummies, we are just tourists, making some notes that may help in a documentary."

"I will not charge much, can explain to you about things many tourists don't know. The history and meaning of the hieroglyphics and much more."

Ayond was confident that he may be an asset to engage. She took a gamble. "As I said, we are tourists come for a holiday to your great country, any extra knowledge about your pyramids and temples would be helpful. Perhaps we can learn more from you, though it is really not necessary. We are a group of six, how much will you charge?"

He promptly said, "Three hundred pound per day, from morning to 4 pm when we close the museum"

"That is too much, will pay you 150 per day, just for a couple of days.

"How about 250."

"175 and that is final," Ayond took out her purse and discretely exposing the stack of notes while bringing out the cash to pay him.

"This is in advance for the two days. We will meet you here tomorrow at 11.

He agreed with the words, "If I am good, you will pay me more?"

"That is to be seen how good you are."

At the hotel bar they chatted generally, tourist stuff. After sometime David complimented Ayond on her clever manoeuvres with the man and how she won him over. "To me he seemed to be very knowledgeable. He is young, ambitious and manageable. We have to be careful, he may be connected with the police or the secret service."

"Won't trust him right away, I have to use my mental power to read his mind." She said and looked at Aishtra "You have not said a word. Missing home already?"

"Not at all, quite fascinated with this place. I have seen some of our people inside the museum, but I don't think they have seen me. This is an old country like most places in the Middle East, Jinn are full of them."

"What a day, how about another round before dinner," Jim suggested.

"Why not," Sam put in raising his empty glass and called for service.

# CHAPTER 25

**The next morning** sharp at 11 the team met with the man they have hired. "My name is Saeed," he introduced himself. He shook hands with each of them, likewise they introduce themselves.

Aishtra wore light dark glasses and whispered to Sam "No one can spot me with them on. As long as I behave normal, I am OK."

For the first couple of hours the guide repeated all the sections they had seen the previous days.

"Excuse me Mr Saeed," David looked at him, "How many Mummies are there, must be hundreds."

"There are many, unimportant people are kept in a warehouse, only famous ones are displayed up here."

"You must be having a big warehouse, anything else is kept there?"

"Oh yes many things, stones, furniture and old tools. Many, many items, I will show you one day. I have to get special permission, we have to pay a little bit here and there," he said with a wink of the eye.

That said a lot, meaning 'baksheesh' or a tip!

David understood what the wink meant. He also understood that bribery can do miracles. He looked at Ayond and winked at her. She understood.

"Too early for that yet," she said to David in a low voice.

They changed the subject and began to talk about Cairo by night. Sam interrupted them and requested Saeed as to where they could see a typical Egyptian night show. Saeed explained that there are many places but suggested, "Some of them are not good to take ladies, but I can think of one place that all of you might enjoy."

"You can count us out, Aishtra and I, would rather stay in. You boys go ahead and have a nice time."

"Then I will select a typical Egyptian show, you men will enjoy, it starts at 11 and goes on until 4 in the morning, I will reserve a table and meet you at the hotel at 10:30."

After Saeed left, Ayond looked at Sam, "That was very clever of you to test Saeed, and won him over like all tourist do. But don't do anything that will jeopardise our mission. Avoid talking about mummies and pyramids, just talk about girls and drinks, study Saeed and see what kind of a person he is. Can he be trusted and so on?"

At the appointed hour all four men were at the hotel lounge, Saeed was already there and greeted them warmly. Without wasting any time all got into a taxi.

The driver had Arabic music at full blast, with the car taking off like a bullet. They exchanged glances and requested Saeed to lower the volume of the music.

The car meandered through crowed street almost hitting pedestrians and smashing into cars.

"Don't be afraid, unless we drive that way we will take two hours to reach. He is a good driver, he is my cousin and good driving experience. He only had two major accidents in five years."

Nobody said a word, they had their fingers crossed. Daniel crossed himself every time the taxi missed a pedestrian.

Soon they stopped at a well-lit entrance with posters showing girls with belly dancing outfits, with maximum exposure of their bodies.

They entered with Saeed leading the way. He said something to a waiter and he welcomed them in Arabic and broken English. "Welcome, welcome your table in front, VIP table."

The table was right in front close to a slightly raised platform where the show would be. They settled down, looked around them, the place was half full. Saeed explained that most people come late. The waiter appeared again with a bottle of Scotch, empty glasses, ice and a jug of water. David asked for soda water and to take away the water. He whispered looking at his companions, "Avoid drinking water in public places may not be safe."

Saeed acting as the host, unscrewed the bottle of Scotch poured generously into each glass, "Hold it," Jim said putting hand on top of the glass, "Don't want to be drunk, the night is still young."

"Cheers," Saeed lifted his glass and took a large gulp.

David looked at Saeed and poured more soda water into his glass. He picked the bottle of Scotch and placed it in front of him. A precaution not to allow Saeed to over indulge.

Jim and Sam were talking, "Never been to such a place. They say Egypt, Syria and Lebanon are the only Middle Eastern country with no hang ups, but the rest have double standards. The rich consume by the gallons in closed doors though it is prohibited, and if a common person is caught drinking, he is lashed in public and a foreigner is lashed and deported."

"I didn't know that," Jim expressed surprise, "What kind of justice is that?"

David politely conversed with Saeed about how lucky they were to have him as a guide and greatly impressed with the Egyptian hospitality. Daniel was listening in and asked Saeed about the freedom of religion.

"Muslims, Christians and Jews are free to worship, no problem. The Christian Orthodox Church is very old and all respect each other. I take you to one of our very old churches if you want."

"That will be very nice of you, if we have time, would surely like to visit."

And so the five hit it well. From subject to subject they talked, the lights began to dim. The uproar of the now full hall was dying out. Pin drop silence griped the air, all eyes were focused on to the brightly lit stage. Music began softly with a gentle female voice accompanying it.

The music faded and a lady in long black speckled mirror like glitter on her dress walked in. The sound of drums and trumpets announcing her entrance erupted, followed by a thunderous applaud and whistles from the audience.

"She is one of our famous singers," Saeed explained.

She said a few words and the crowed exclaimed. She began to sing, the audience calmed down and her voice filled the hall with an occasional bursts of applause and appreciative utterances.

After a brief interval another song followed. It was soft and sounded romantic. The audience listened in complete silence.

The attendants busied themselves serving, brought grilled chicken and sheesh kababs, and salads to go with it.

The lights on the staged began to flash with musical accompaniment, it got louder as a troupe of girls entered in a dancing display, they were dressed in colourful attires, each holding a tambourine with hands drumming and some bodily movements. The atmosphere was beginning to be explosive with musical fervour. They girls danced in concentric circles changing to the figure of eight and more complicated twists and turns. The lights dimmed further, the clapping from the audience encouraged the dancers to be more frenzy. It continued and did as the audience wished for. Discretely, they moved back to the stage with the music dying out.

The lights became brighter for people to enjoy their meals.

Saeed had reclaimed the bottle of Scotch from David and was pouring generously. They consumed the grills and ordered for more.

Shortly after, the lights dimmed again, with soft flashing coloured spot lights from the top; dancers with minimal see through clothing, exposing their belly buttons entered with the sound of flute and soft drum beats, wriggling their bodies, to suit the tempo.

They came to the table where Saeed was, they danced, rubbing against each of them, placing their palms on to their heads ruffling their hair and moved on to another table.

To add more to the already explosive ambiance, eight additional dancers entered. Some in the audience joined in and danced. Saeed encourage his companions to do the same, but abstained. Saeed joined in for a short while. The hours passed, it was time for the final act.

All the dancers exited, leaving one, the light focussed on her, she sang with a warm soft voice, accompanied by acrobatic hand and hip motions, mesmerising the on looker to the level of complete silence, allowing her seductive voice rule supreme.

It was nearly 4 am when the show ended. Saeed led the way out, disappeared for a while and returned with a taxi. It was his cousin's, he had told to come back for them.

# CHAPTER 26

**The team assembled** at the hotel lounge, Ayond nursed a hot cup of tea while the others busied talking. After a full report of the previous night's experience at the belly dancers show was recounted by David, he endorsed Saeed as a person may be willing to help.

"To me he can be valuable to our endeavour. Being an employee of the museum, may have an excess to the warehouse he talked about, in which countless items are stored. I asked him to join us at midday, in the hotel, not at the museum.

"I trust your judgement David, but we must not move too quickly. Let me handle him today, and put some leading questions."

It was past midday and no sign of Saeed. "Perhaps last night was too much for him. He must be fast asleep somewhere in the museum," Sam said helping himself to some tea. He spoke too soon, from a distance he saw Saeed rushing towards them.

"Sorry, I am late, but my uncle woke me up early and asked me to do some errands for him which I could not refuse. It is part of my job."

"Part of museum job?" Sam asked.

"Yes, had to deliver a few things."

"Does your uncle work there with you?"

"Yes, he is the Deputy Director."

"Of the museum?" David could not believe what he heard.

"Yes, I work directly under him," Saeed said and added, "He is very tough task master."

Ayond was more than pleased and offered him a cup of tea.

The stage was set for her next move.

"Tell me Saeed how many years have you been working in the museum?"

"Nearly ten years, had one year's training in the UK and mostly field work with my uncle. He taught me everything even to read Hieroglyphics and many other things."

"Aren't you missing work showing us round?" Ayond questioned.

"No, I told my uncle that I am guiding some tourist and they pay me good money. He encourages me to do such jobs only with Westerners not locals, they pay well. Our salaries are small, I make 1500 pounds a month that is about 400 American dollar.

"Only this morning I ask him to give me a week's leave so that I can be with you day and night, if necessary."

"Only day will do, had enough for one night. If you know what I mean," Sam said, looking at the rest with a smile.

Ayond was keen to talk to him privately. She had the nephew of the second highest authority of the Egyptian Museum. The chances were, that he might have some clue or information to the devise's where about.

Not to create any suspicion she started, "When we have time, I would like to visit the old market place and buy some souvenirs."

She turned to David, why don't you all go to the concierge and fix a time for sightseeing." He got the hint.

She wanted some time with Saeed. A bell boy came pacing with a card, on it was "Madam Ayond", he kept on repeating, "Yes," she called, he told her, two gentlemen waiting at the reception and want meet her.

"Excuse me Saeed, I will be back soon, help yourself to a cup of tea."

She met the men the Guardian had sent and met them at the airport.

Returned to Saeed, "Sorry, to keep you waiting, tell me Saeed, the pyramids always fascinated me. Can't imagine they were built by men using simple tools thousands of years ago."

Saeed thought for a while as how to reply that question, "Yes, they say built by slaves, many of them, but I don't believe that, they were Egyptian labour."

"Anything special found inside the pyramid, such as special manuscripts that cannot be deciphered. I am very fascinated by the genius of their construction and astronomical wisdom of the time, the alignment with the stars." She did not want to get into

175

technical details. As a casual tourist one is not to have too much of 'technical' knowledge.

She rephrased her question. "The greatness of the Egyptian architects must had been such that they must had left some records in the form of text or artefacts as to how they were built." she was repeating herself, she wanted to hear something that might lead to the discovery of an object the authorities may have found and hid away.

Saeed did not understand the question. But in his keenness to help, he replied, "We are very rich in artefacts, all sorts, some of which we do not understand."

"Why can't you get foreign experts, Germans, French or British? They will be able to help, two heads are better than one, if you know what I mean."

"We always consult them, but there are some we cannot show them, they are very precious and mysterious."

"Nothing can be mysterious, after all they were made many years ago by Egyptians," Ayond qualified.

"Yes, but there are items too sophisticated for that age, for example," he stopped and made comical gestures with his hand, like a ball or a square, "For example, there was that thing which looked like a box, made of metal, could not be made by Egyptians, thousands of years ago. It has the modern technological feature. At first we suspected that some foreign people had put it in there, as a gag. Our Director, ridiculed the idea, because it was inserted deep inside a sealed cavity, at the time the Pyramid was built. It had to be drilled open."

That was the magic word Ayond wanted to hear. She was on the right path. She was thinking of a new strategy.

She changed the subject, not to show any eagerness, "How a boat ride on the Nile, late this afternoon. Love to cruise and enjoy some sunshine."

"I can arrange that, how about 4 in the afternoon."

It was not a sail boat, which Ayond had in mind, but motorized, line with mattresses and cushions, and a decorative canvas roof top. Two men, one at the wheel and the other busied himself with the engine.

Minutes into the Nile, Saeed produced bottles of beer and handed each one a napkin, from a basket he served sandwiches prepared by the hotel.

Cruised down the Nile, enjoyed the sights of people milling on either side, some on donkeys, or escorting goats, cattle or camels. Small mud houses, outside women busied cooking on charcoal or wood fires. The scene was of another period in time, compared to the cosmopolitan splendour of modern Cairo.

Just before sunset, the boat headed back to where they started, not far from the Hotel. Decided to sit on the benches that lined the bank, and enjoy the setting sun.

On a bench Ayond sat next to Saeed and David. On another, Sam and Aishtra with his arm stretched resting on the back of the bench. Jim and Daniel stood by the bank admiring the hazy horizon the setting sun offered.

Ayond talked in general about the greatness of the Egyptian heritage, and the possibilities of finding more wonders, from their ancient past. All this, was to gradually lead up to the box found in the Pyramid. "Talking about wonders, you said something about a box found in a Pyramid, was it really of a modern origin, what happened to it?"

"Nothing," Saeed said casually, "It will just remain and gather dust, and as we are very secretive people, especially with thing we do not understand, do not show it to foreigners, they will come out with theories that may contradict our religious value."

"Very true, but at the same time, are the authorities not inquisitive to find out, at least in a private capacity, what it is, who put it there and for what purpose?" Then as an eager tourist would react, "How I would like to see that box. Just to touch it, a relic thousands of years old."

"Only for you, as you are very pleasant people, different from others, I may be able to arrange for that, give me time to think. I can't ask my uncle, he will never agree. But there is another way, it will cost you some money to pay here and there."

"What do mean, here and there."

"The people guarding it."

"Isn't that dangerous. What if they are caught?"

"With money everything is possible."

"You do what you have to, tell me when ready." Ayond had scored.

She would finally have her hands on the device they have come for. But the question remained, how to take it away from Saeed.

"Can he and the others be bribed to give it to us," she thought hard.

She invited Saeed to join them for dinner. Before that they met at the bar and talked informally on subjects other than the box. It was Saeed who after a few drinks, became more forthright, and almost in a whisper, "Regarding the box, if I pay the guards a thousand Egyptian pounds, you can see the box for one hour."

"That will be great Saeed," then jokingly putting her hand on his, making a funny face, "How much more will it cost to have it more than one hour, say permanently."

"What do mean permanently, you mean to take it?"

Ayond looked squarely on his face and holding his hand tight, "Yes."

He freed his hand, stood up and scratched his head.

"You mean to take it away that is impossible, customs will catch you and you will go to jail. Why do you want to take such a risk for a worthless box and what will you do with it?"

"Just to keep it as a souvenir."

"Many foreigners steal our treasure, but they pay too much."

She was leading him to the next question. "How much this box will cost."

"You are not serious. You are respectable tourist, in fact all of you, why bring trouble to yourselves over something that has no artistic design."

Ayond gave a gentle smile, "Because it is so, worthless old box that is why. We foreigners sometimes are crazy, just collect things that are worthless as a decoration piece in our house. At least it will have a home, better than gathering dust and forgotten in your museum."

She allowed Saeed a few minutes to digest what she had just said. She busied herself as if searching for something in her purse. David was watching what Ayond was up to.

Saeed broke the impasse, "Are you serious, it is a big risk for me and all of you. Our jails are not as good as you have in London. There are mice, lizards and much mosquitoes."

She did not react, but continued to look at the setting sun. Turning to Saeed, put her hand on to his, "Don't you worry, we nor you will be caught, as you said, with money everything is possible."

Saeed thought for a long minute, "I think you are serious. You want the worthless box as a souvenir. A few thousand dollars, not for me, for the guards. I am not sure if can be done, but will try."

"And a few thousand for you, for your trouble," Ayond winked and gave him a wide smile.

# CHAPTER 27

**The next day** they met at the hotel lounge waiting for Saeed, just before noon, Ayond briefed the team what would be their next roll.

"When Saeed comes act normal, keep talking among yourselves, and look busy. Perhaps he and I may go to the bar and do our business. He is not supposed to know that you all are on this, perhaps later.

"We do not want to embarrass him in any way. I will set a date as to when he could deliver the box, once done, plan our next move to retrieve the other item from the Sphinx. It is important as it is a part of the device to insert the medallion into it and activate it. Once the operation is completed, we depart the same day.

"Aishtra will take both items and using her Jinn skills, depart for home. On her arrival, she will hand over the items to the Guardian, and call us. The two gentlemen the Guardian had sent will arrange to put us on a flight the same day."

Jim pointed out, "You are a very lucky woman, and it came too easy, only in films this can happen; not in real life. I hope we are not being set up."

"I thought of that Jim, actually we are lucky to come across a person like Saeed. He happened to be there, and approached us as he may have done countless times earning on the side from tourist. It was my leading questions that did the trick."

"I fully agree to that deduction. The correct word put at the appropriate time can do wonders, and you Ayond, have achieved it," Sam expounded.

Saeed arrived with two bouquets of flowers, he gave them to Ayond and Aishtra. After a brief conversation, Ayond took Saeed aside, and the rest moved away.

"This morning I made all the arrangements, it will cost 10,000 American Dollars, five to each. They will leave the keys behind while they go for lunch. Someone whom they trust will open the room where the box is kept and take it to a place where I can find it. You don't have to pay this other man, the guards will each pay him $ 500 from their money.

"You have to tell me one day in advance when you want it, pay me the money and the next day shall deliver."

"Excellent Saeed, be careful, don't get into any trouble." Ayond said softly showing concern.

"The arrangement I have made, is fool proof, knowing our system nobody will miss it, at least for some time, God knows for how long."

"You are very smart Saeed, someday I will contact you to bring you to the UK and find you a good job. As agreed, I will pay you the money a day before the delivery. This is our secret, nobody knows about it."

Ayond could not be a happier person. How it worked out, *it* was sheer luck.

Her next move was the Sphinx but only on the day she pays Saeed.

After Saeed parted, they all congratulated her on her achievement and it was decided to enjoy the rest of the day.

Jim again pointed out, "Not being a pessimist, what if the box he is referring to is not the device we are looking for? You would lose the money on a worthless item, and start all over again."

"That is a possibility, it is a calculated risk I had to take; but in all fairness, I am convinced that it is what I am looking for. The way he described the box and its make, it is not an ordinary container, but looks like one. Let's wait and see.

"For a little distraction from our current suspenseful wait, we will plan a visit to the Sphinx tomorrow, and have on the spot looksee. Plan as to how to tackle our next strategic venture.

"Most likely our visit is coming to an end soon, why not go out and have the best Cairo can offer, you may not get another chance. I will spend the rest of the day in my room," Ayond concluded.

With help of the concierge, each made their arrangements.

Jim and Daniel decided to go out to a cabaret and lose themselves.

Sam and Aishtra booked for a quiet place to dine and dance.

David decided to stay and keep Ayond company.

After they all left for their rendezvous, David and Ayond sat at the bar, loosened up and began to talk about their lives.

David spoke of the good and happy days he spent with his wife, "She was a wonderful person, caring, loving and worked hard to keep our house blissful. One morning she complained of an acute pain in her abdomen, an illness could not be diagnosed. She passed away in a matter of days.

"My sons are well settled and I am now in good hands, can't ask for more.

Ayond held his hand firmly, "You are in good hand for sure, and I am always there for you.

"Now let me tell you somethings about me. I have told you, I was born on Earth, my father and mother worked with Guardian and Supreme High, they were also born here. Surprisingly I met a man in my younger days, who looked and behaved like Sam. We fell in love, being adventurous and always helping people in need, on one occasion when on a pleasure trip on a boat, took a life threatening risk to save a child from drowning who accidently fell into the waters, infested with shark. He rescued him and in the process of lifting him to be hauled up to the boat a shark got him and dragged him under. He was not seen again. That happened just months before we were to be wed.

"When I met Sam the first time, I thought of seeing a ghost. A reincarnation, but I don't believe in that's stuff. I liked him and somehow I knew inwardly that we would meet again. I did not have that feeling for him as my lost beloved one. I treated him as a friend.

"With you David, I do have a very special feelings. I shall always treasure it."

David got up and asked her for a dance. At one point he drew her close and kissed her.

They had dinner and retired to the lounge, spent in conversation when they saw Sam and Aishtra walk in.

"How was your evening," Ayond asked.

"Just wonderful, too tired, must go to bed."

"We too must end the night, we have a long day tomorrow," Ayond said getting up.

The next day the four met at dining room for breakfast.

"I haven't seen Jim and Daniel, must recuperating after last night's indulgences," Sam was mocking.

"Leave them alone, they are grown men," Ayond said, then added, "Sam get them ready to meet at 3 in the afternoon to visit the Sphinx."

They reached the Sphinx and settled on a raised area, looked at it, Ayond thoughts went back to the archives, the recordings of what led her predecessors to come to that design.

She visualised the carving of a large block of rock jutting out conspicuously on a barren terrain, the digging around its base to give it the body shape of a lion, and the modelling of a human head. The front resting position of the legs had to be improvised, mostly hollow from the inside. "And that is where that bit I am looking would be."

Her thoughts were interrupted by Aishtra calling, she and the rest were descending to the Sphinx.

The place was filled with tourists and security. "Our excavation has to be at night and get rid of the guard somehow." She thought.

Just to families themselves with the place, they decide to walk around and mingle with the tourists and get inside the narrow corridor. The crowd was thing out, soon they were the only ones inside. A guard told them to hurry as closing time is in 30 minutes. David thanked the guard and passed on a 20 pound note. The guard was overwhelmed and became more accommodating, allowed them to stay a little longer.

The key to get things done is always the 'Baksheesh', a tip.

Ayond went to a section very near the entrance and pointed to a rectangular design of hieroglyphics, "We have to cut around this and a passage will lead us to a chamber under the right arm of the lion, in a large stone container, the part needed lies within.

"The question is how to do away with the guards and dig into the wall. I don't think money will work, we have to figure out another way," Sam remarked.

"Digging is not a problem, I have brought with me an instrument like a laser gun, undetectable by x-ray, just shows a plain metal object like a ruler, that is we got it through customs, and makes very subdued whining sound when activated. I will cut around the hieroglyphic section and it will be the doorway to walk through the lion's paw. Think of a way to get rid of the guards."

Back at the hotel, they had to come out with a solution. Jim came out with an idea.

"Drug the guards, at night nobody will miss them."

Aishtra was listening attentively. She interrupted, "While we were leaving the place I notice a couple of Jinn in the area. Now I remembered that at around dusk Jinn come out and occupy the places where no or few humans venture. If you wish, I can make contact and see if they could help us."

"In what way," David asked.

"In frightening the guards. They can appear as ugly demons."

"A good idea. Why can't you do it, why involve outsiders. It may harm our mission."

"Yes, why not you Aishtra you are a Jinn or have you forgotten your tricks," Ayond was teasing.

"No I have not, it is something you do not forget. We are born with it, I can attempt it now and have a sort of rehearsal. She looked at her watch, "It is about seven, right conditions after dusk."

Aishtra opened a window and off she went appeared on the paw, unnoticed slid down towards the entrance. She began to sing. Hearing her, one of the guards walked up, as he got closer she changed her form to a lion.

*H.P. Kabir*

The guard froze for a moment, with a loud yell he ran passed the other guard and shouted for help. The second guard ran after him and held him. "There is a lion on the loose. He was singing too. The place is jinked." He was hysterical.

"Calm down, it must be your imagination, you better go home I will be on duty."

Aishtra returned and to the waiting colleagues, she just said, "It worked perfectly."

# CHAPTER 28

**The next day at 11 pm** they ventured out. The taxi dropped them a few hundred yard from the Sphinx. The driver tried to tell them that there was nothing to see at that late hour, but they just paid him with a generous tip. "This is for you, Baksheesh." The driver thanked them, at the same time said something in Arabic, perhaps, "What a mad lot these foreigners are."

They came just about 50 feet from the Sphinx. Aishtra was asked to go ahead and do her act. She moved slowly with tinkling sound like jingles, the two guards were enjoying some tea, put their cups down and went to investigate. They stopped to see a cow coming towards them. As they were about to turn to go back the cow bellowed a long flame from its mouth, then changed shape to a bull with red bright eyes.

Both guards pretended to walk away nonchalantly, then with a strong yell ran as fast as they could. The team waited for some time to see if they would return back. They did not.

They moved cautiously and entered the passage of the Sphinx. Aishtra was to kept a watch on the outside. She can handle any unwanted visitors.

Ayond took the ruler shaped laser gun and began cutting through the stone. Minutes later the cut slab was given a push and it fell with a loud crash. It broke into several pieces.

They waited if the noise attracted anyone in the vicinity. "All is well," They heard Aishtra voice.

Ayond led the way all held torches. "No one walked this passage for thousands of years."

"The ground, the wall and the ceiling are smooth though slightly damp," Jim noticed running his hand across the wall and ceiling. The passage dipped with a slight incline, at the end of which, lay a square stone container, with a lid 5 inches thick.

Ayond placed a tripod on top of the lid, "It has to be straight and vertical, only then it will work, to ease the weight of the slab." They felt a vibration on to the slab, moments later, she asked them to push. "It is a smaller slab than that of the coffin in Michael house." She removed the tripod and they all pushed. It moved a few inches, with one hard trust, it slid off and fell with a thud on the sandy ground.

All torches flooded the inside to show a small package resting in its centre.

Sam climbed over and jumped in. He picked the package and handed it to Ayond.

She unwrapped it and a V shaped implement with several protruding nail like pins on one side.

"Yes, it is what we want, let's leave quickly, and let the security beat their heads off tomorrow." Retraced their way out, looked around, and the guards nowhere to be seen.

"Who would believe the guards' story, though the damage to the Sphinx could only be attributed to an angry bull with satanic red eyes," Daniel interposed with a bit of humour.

It was after mid night, the area was deserted unlike in the city. The roads empty, a passing truck gave them a ride. They got off on a main street and paid the driver. A passing taxi stopped and asked them if they wanted a ride.

Back at the hotel, Sam and David headed straight to the bar. It was shut. An attendant appeared, Sam pleadingly asked him if he could provide a bottle of Scotch, "We had a tough day, need a drink," While talking took out a few Pound notes and placed into his palm.

The Bakhshes worked, almost in an instant, service was at hand. The bottle and glasses were placed in front of them.

They were joined by Ayond and the rest. After a while, the waiter requested them to take the bottle to their room, as it was getting late.

They slept soundly, completely oblivious of their earlier exploit.

Early morning Ayond was up and about, called Saeed and asked him to come over.

Within the hour he arrived, paid him the money and told her that he would bring the box the next day at noon. She then contacted the two men sent by the Guardian, to arrange for their travel back to London, the next day. Most flights to Europe leave late at night, had sufficient time to get organized.

She called all to meet at her room. They sat comfortably facing Ayond who was fully stretched on a long sofa, "Mission successfully accomplished, we leave tomorrow night."

There were burst of felicitations.

The next day she waited in her room waiting for Saeed. It was near to midday, her anxiety mounted. Switched on the television, showed Syrian and Israeli clashes. A brief report on the virus, which did not sound encouraging. Switched it off. Thought of Saeed, "What if he fails," Kept repeating to herself.

A knock at the door sent her running and opened it. Saeed stood with a large grin on his face, "I have it," He said. Ayond threw herself on him and gave him a bear hug.

She took the box in her hand and examined it. More relaxed she said, "This will rest in the most prestigious place you can think off. Thank you so much." She further examined it, and knew that it was the device sought for.

Saeed noticed the packed suit case near the door, "Are you leaving?" He asked politely.

"Yes Saeed, something urgent has turned up back home, we have to leave."

"Will miss all of you, have been good tourist, hope to meet you some day, may be you come back for collecting more souvenirs, the one you have is a big risk, but will make a nice decoration piece." He said with a smile.

Ayond handed Saeed an envelope, "This is something extra, treat it as a gift. Soon I will contact you and be ready to join us in the UK, get your visa beforehand, and must not tell anyone.

Ayond came closer to Saeed, "You just act normal and do your job routinely as if nothing has happened. Try to see less of your uncle if possible and don't say anything to your wife."

"I am not married. I am a free man, my parents passed away years back, with no responsibility to anyone."

"Sorry to hear about your parents, you are a good person and keep it that way," she comforted him.

With tears in his eye, he moved towards Ayond, embraced her and kissed her hands. "I will not forget you, like a family to me." With those words he left.

She wasted no time, called her impatiently waiting colleagues and forthwith they came in.

"I have it!" She exclaimed then added soberly, "Saeed left with tears in his eyes, became emotionally attached to us"

Each one of them held the device and examined it.

"The symbols and buttons must mean something, do you know how it works?" Jim asked.

"To some extent I do, but the Guardian can do better. It will be him and the Supreme High who will read the message and translate to English for the world to understand. They will decide when, how and where it will be read. Let's not worry about that right now, must get the devices to them as soon as Aishtra is ready.

"When can you leave?"

"Just after dusk, best time to travel," Aishtra replied.

Just at sunset Aishtra got herself ready for the journey back home in the Jinn fashion of travel. She had no luggage, just a small packet with the two devices. . She slung it across her shoulder and held it tight. Opened the door to the balcony, "Will call you in a few moments," Aishtra said as she leapt off the balcony gradually turning invisible. They shouted with one voice, "Bon voyage."

They sat silently and flipped through magazines, waiting for Aishtra's call.

Minutes were like hours, time moved sluggishly. The telephone rang, broke the silence. They jumped up and waited for Ayond to answer.

"Glad to hear your voice, you have already handed them to the Guardian, excellent. We will now go down and check out, see you tomorrow, until then bye from all of us." Ayond gave a sigh of relief, and hurriedly they all went down to the lobby.

Shortly after, the two men entered, and escorted them out of the hotel. At the airport, taken to the VIP lounge, the flight took off on time.

# CHAPTER 29

**The Guardian and the Supreme High** had agreed that on a certain date to be fixed with the British Special Department handling the affairs of the aliens, who would announcement the discovery of a machine left by extra-terrestrial visitors millenniums ago with a message to mankind.

The Supreme High had translated the text within the device which was in their language after its assembly and the insertion of the medallion, and rerecorded it within. He also added a message of his own.

The Guardian sat at the head of the table with Ayond and Aishtra on his sides. He looked at the team and stood up, "I congratulate all of you for a job well done," then he sat down and continued, "The next steps are not going be easy; we have to get the British Government involved as we are guests here, they will be the ones to make the initial move. Ayond has been the link with them and in the next day or two she will contact the person in charge of that special department, as far as we know no one else in the government knows of its existence, and that person will brief the Prime Minister.

"After that we will invite the Prime Minister and the person in charge to our facility and show them what we have here. All these years no one had visited or asked us to inspect it. All in good faith and reciprocally we have done the same, never interfered with their internal or external activities. Occasionally we did give indirect help on certain issues, making them believe it is on their efforts. It is a great nation, a well-deserved song by Thomas Arne, 'Rule Britannia'," The Guardian concluded.

There was pin drop silence for a while. It was David who raised his hand, "Forgive me for butting in, what about other Governments, like the United States, Canada, Germany and so on, who is going to brief them."

Ayond addressed his question by saying, "The British government, and the United Nations will be the ones, and perhaps to other world governments and the world as a whole."

"Will the announcement be made through the UN using the device?," Sam put in looking at Ayond.

"It will probably be the best way."

After replying questions put by the team, the Guardian got up, wished them well in the difficult tasks that lay ahead.

Next was a visit to the Supreme High, with the Guardian accompanying. "This time there were no security checks," Ayond clarified. They stood in front of the highest authority in the facility.

The Supreme High came to life with all the little pin head lights fully active. "Welcome to you all. I want to congratulate you on an excellent job done in Egypt. David, Jim, Sam and Daniel you have proven yourselves, you four can come and see me whenever you wish, and there will be no barriers between us.

"I have some plans for you, we'll talk about it some other time, for now, Ayond is fully authorised to conduct what is to be done, I wish you all well, until next time." He asked the Guardian to stay, "Say good bye to your guests and come back."

The Guardian escorted them to the door, and said, "I have not seen the Supreme High so pleased with humans, he always had some reservation. But you four have scored well. I am equally delighted."

The next day Ayond came with disturbing news. "The virus in India and South East Asia has mutated into a something that looks like a cross breed between a beetle and a locust, about two inches long, mercilessly devouring vegetation and human flesh. Unless it is stopped, humanity, plants and whatever is edible, will wipe be out. The chances are, this menace may mutate into some other form, deadlier than its predecessor. No chemical or antidote has been found to eradicate this threat. It somehow, helps it to mutate further. We have designated a group of scientists to work on its entomology.

"On another note, I have contacted the man in charge of our welfare in the Special Department, and he agreed to meet me tomorrow."

It would be Ayond's first meeting with him since he took over from his predecessor who retired some years ago and whom she knew well.

At his office, Ayond narrated the whole story and the importance of telling the world, "Not by us, but by the British Government or a world body like the United Nations. Perhaps it will bring some diversion from the warring factions and bring people together to their senses."

"Since my taking charge, I contemplated in contacting you, but voted against it. But now, as you have come with an interesting offer, will do my best to help you. Will surely have a try at it, though may not work out well, world politics is a nasty business. I shall brief the Prime Minister, who like others before him do not have the faintest idea of your existence, not only that, and living in our back yard so to speak."

"Thank you Mr. Steven Windsor, I will wait for your call." Ayond said.

"My friends call me Steve, and would appreciate, if you do so," He said.

"Yes Steve, and by the way, should the Prime Minister agree to meet me, I suggest that you and him come over to our premises, he will meet the highest authorities among us. You may have read our files, all is in there."

"That would be interesting, will do my best." Steve said.

Ayond was pleased, informed the Guardian and her team.

To her joy, it was the next day Steve called, "The Prime Mister was thrilled, and asked me to convey his acceptance to visit you, and took the liberty to suggest, Saturday, about midday."

"Thank you Steve, please make sure only your security men accompany you."

She explained the drill to her team, "After their meeting with the Guardian and the Supreme High, will bring them to David's room, shall make the arrangement to sit outside in the Garden. Steve is a pleasant man, will enjoy chatting with you.

On Saturday, all arrangement were in place.

The guests arrived. Took them to Guardian and the Supreme High, only Ayond and Aishtra accompanied.

David and his colleagues waited in the garden dressed for the occasion, Ayond entered with the Prime Minister, Steve and Aishtra.

The Prime Minister, in his late forties, after shaking hands, stood and looked up and around, admiring the settings, "I wouldn't have believed that we are down under, forgive the expression, had I not descended through those stairs.

"It must have taken some effort to get it done. When was it built?"

Steve promptly answered, "Sir, I have all the details, will pass them to you to read at leisure"

The next half hour socialized and was happy to meet the four British subject, David and his friend as part of an alien family.

Again Steve explained, "Only recently they came into the picture, we have received their identities sent by Ayond, and we have registered them. You heard the praises and appreciations the Supreme High had for them, we should be proud."

"Love to spend more time to hear you stories, perhaps soon, some other time."

The meeting ended with Steve going to each of them, and added, "As you are part of this Facility, I am there to help, day or night. You are in good hands and likewise shall be the same from us."

They left, Ayond and Aishtra returned, the sat and looked at the four waiting for some speak. They reciprocated by staring at both wanting them to begin.

Finally Ayond said, almost shouting, "What happened to your hospitality, can I have a cup of tea!"

Sam rushed, and brought two cups, placed one in front of her and the other to Aishtra.

David politely said, "What about us." Looking at Sam. He obliged.

"That was great, the Prime Minister and Steve were more than impressed, promised to do all they can to help getting the message in the device heard by world leaders.

"The Prime Minister said something to the effect that we, the aliens, had as much right to be on this planet as any other human being, having lived here much before the time of your written history. What I liked was when he said to the Guardian with a bit of humour, "It's about time you all got your British citizenships."

"What will be our next move?" Jim asked.

"No next move until we hear from Steve. Meanwhile, concentrate on the Middle East situation and the virus epidemic.

"The message, if and when read, may fall on deaf ears, the war will continue, with more deaths and destruction, and the virus unstoppable. We, as outsiders will only watch the inevitable demise of life on this beautiful world."

"That is a pessimistic view Ayond, with all your sciences can't you get rid of a tiny insect," David interjected.

"It may be tiny, but nature has it reasons to make it immune for a purpose, perhaps it's meant to be, but there is always a weak spot in everything. Unless we find out what makes tick and what its weaknesses are, nothing can be done.

"The last scenes from China and Mongolia are horrendous, this carnivorous beast stripping flesh off animals and people alike.

"It has crept into Afghanistan and eastern Iran, and progressing fast into western China, soon will enter Tibet.

"I wonder if the weather has anything to do with its fast dispersal. This year we are experiencing an extra ordinary heat wave, it is possible that would be the catalyst for its path to warmer grounds. If so, the Middle East and soon into Africa." Ayond observed.

David suggested that on a map, colour the areas the virus has moved into, perhaps avoiding terrains its does not like the smell of.

"A very good idea David, let's go to the library and get started," Ayond said got up, followed by all.

At the library a world political map was spread and with a red marker outlined the areas infected by the virus. Another suggestion came from Daniel, "How about the present weather conditions in those areas."

Aishtra made a phone call and gave instructions to provide the weather charts of Asia and Africa for that month.

Studying the weather charts and comparing them with infected areas on the map, they clearly noticed that it has not gone beyond Nepal, but has moved east to Myanmar, Thailand east into China. From the west, to Afghanistan and Iran. Stopped east of the Tibetan Plateau. Went around it and into Mongolia and further west into central Asia.

"Why has it avoided northern Nepal and went around the Tibetan Plateau," David put a question.

Jim scratched his head and put in comically, "Perhaps it is afraid of heights or the air is too thin."

"It makes sense Jim," David responded. How about Afghanistan and Iran that is a mountainous area. Let's have look at their weather chart."

The weather chart showed a warm summer.

"Some parts of that area are facing a warm summer, I tend to agree with Jim, not about heights or air, but hinted at avoiding those area, and weather could be a factor.

"Aishtra, can you please arrange for the daily weather reports, and mark in red the progress of the virus." David requested.

They returned to their rooms fatigued and gloomy, thinking about the virus, Daniel read the Holy Book and prayed for a miracle.

# CHAPTER 30

**Three days have passed** and no new from Steve. The team busied themselves at the library working on the progress of the virus. Nothing concrete has come out from the weather analysis.

The news on television said the same story over and over again about the raging war in the Middle East. More countries have joined in, taking sides irrationally. The Suez Canal littered with sunken ships caused a blockade of a major trade route.

The Super powers gave lip service. They were cautious, might trigger a world catastrophe.

"The Americans suggested to bomb the virus infected areas. The Russian warned them not to. The Chinese have used flame throwers in some parts without much success, caused havoc among the population.

The Indians used boiling water using water cannons. It was a failure and helped its manifestation more vigorously. Besides people, animal and plants, it devoured wooden structure and cables.

Steve called Ayond and told her that the Super powers have not yet responded and the Prime Minister will speak to the U.N. Secretary General.

Ayond conveyed his message to the Guardian.

The Guardian reported back to Ayond that the Supreme High approved the British decision to deal directly with the United Nations, and as for the virus, considered their efforts to follow the weather patterns, as it was a logical endeavour.

She in turn advised her team of the Supreme High's comments, but added, "He also said something about what the Supreme High had said to him, about, after making the announcement to the world, we will discuss our future plans on this planet, and I could not comprehend what he meant.

Those remarks got Ayond thinking, in so many years the question of our stay on Earth was never an issue.

"Yes sir, what are your plans, why are you thinking of leaving good old Earth, go where, to Urna, our surrogate planet which we abandoned thousands of years ago. Who would welcome us there, we would be like fish out of water." Ayond was reminiscing sullenly alone in her room, almost talking.

Days passed and Steve did not contact her.

Meanwhile, Aishtra continued to follow the weather patterns and the virus, which she has coined a name for it, called it the *creature*. It hit Iraq, Syria, Jordan, Israel, Saudi Arabia and Egypt. In a matter of days would enter into the Sudan and beyond. With Asia and Africa combined total deaths would rise into billions. Another recent report added Turkey to the list, Europe would be next.

Ayond was not as vibrant as always, she had the worrying thought of leaving earth as indicated by the Supreme High, but her position as Grand Master and third in command of the aliens, had to act and behave normally.

The virus or the creature as Aishtra had named it, was a blessing in disguise, on the battle fields of the war torn Middle East, it played havoc on both sides. Soared in a swarm, obscured the sun, and descended like missiles on the now disorderly and confused combatants, threw away their weapons and ran madly on all direction. The few that were lucky to take shelter, felt that it was the wrath of God to punish them for their acts of war. Mosques were packed with men women and children, asking for salvation. Sheep and goats were sacrificed as an atonement.

"At least they thought it that way, we will have peace for some time, and give us a break to conduct our programme.

Aishtra continued with her task, the virus had spread throughout the countries bordering the Mediterranean Sea.

Steve came to meet with the Guardian and Ayond. His report was discouraging. "The Prime Minister spoke confidentially to some our close allies, but for some reason or the other their reaction was not encouraging.

"On the other hand, the U.N. Secretary General was more positive, suggested to come to New York, two weeks from now, he would be able to arrange a special session to host an '*Out of the World Gathering*', as he put it. Will contact you two days before departure, and please include those wonderful men I met at your facility, A special plane will be at our disposal." With those words, he left.

Meanwhile, the team with Aishtra continued to follow the virus's areas of assault.

Jim thoughtfully indicted that the virus is susceptible to weather conditions. "As you can see on the map, this menace has avoided the cooler regions, it is worth investigating. Send someone to Tibet, have on the spot inspection, and see where the line beyond which their advances halted."

"Thank you Jim, it is worth looking into that assumption. But time is a factor, it take weeks if not a month to visit and return with samples," David said.

"Not really, can be done in an hour, max." Aishtra spoke softly.

"How," Jim asked.

"You all are forgetting what a Jinn is capable of," Aishtra reminded.

"Aishtra you are saviour, get us a sample, several if possible." David requested.

Before her departure met with Ayond at her office and took her approval.

While they waited at the library, busied themselves perusing though books.

Daniel sat and began, almost talking to himself, but audible, "She is an angel in human form, correction, Jinn form. Come to think of, perhaps they were the ones that appeared and disappeared, guided some of us, in the form of supernatural visitation." He stopped, then added, "God forgive me, and meant no offence, just thinking.

They looked at him, eyes focussed.

Sam was appreciative, "Daniel, I tend to agree, don't feel sorry, there are many phenomena that we do not understand and attribute them to heavenly miracles. With time, all these occurrences will be explained rationally. I am a believer in the paranormal, in fact living in it, why not in what you had conjectured."

With Aishtra's apparition forming at one end of the room, they left their seats stood in wonder at was enfolding before them.

Second later she spoke.

"What I saw, it is a clear cut evidence that this villain does not like the cold," putting a package on to the table. "At a certain point on the plateau, many of them lay scattered, frozen dead."

Ayond was called and she asked some of the technical staff to come over. Dressed with appropriate clothing, carefully opened the package. With professional skill, picked the muted beetle-locust insect and put it on a tray. It looked innocent and harmless.

"Any chance of it reviving to back to life, after defrosting?" Ayond was curious.

"No Madame, after we do an autopsy, will burn them. Will keep one or two in a sealed glass container in the lab." A technician said.

"Now we know their weak spot, but how are we going freeze them?" Sam asked.

David put in thoughtfully, "Artificial snow can be an answer, but can it be made in such a large quantity to cover millions of square miles?

Ayond responded, "Why not David, we have the means, some of our ships are equipped to do the job. Technically, it is a simple procedure; the volume to drop will depend on the location, hot areas like in desert conditions will be more, to last many days and less in moderate places.

"Thank you all for your input, as we have the answer to deal with that situation, we will leave it aside for the time being and concentrate on our mission at the United Nations."

Back in David's room they gathered, some went out to the garden and relaxed with a glass of beer.

Days later, Steve called Ayond. Their departure to New York would be the day after.

# CHAPTER 31

**Steve accompanied** by three gentlemen dressed in dark grey suites arrived at the Facility to pick up Ayond and her team. He handed each of them a plastic card, "These are your IDs during your stay in New York, and I have also made your passports which will remain with one of my men." He said.

They boarded a private executive jet and took off.

At New York airport two men came to the plane and escorted them to the hotel.

Ayond's and Aishtra took out the device, tested it and placed it in the safe deposit box available in the suite.

The next day at eight in the morning left for the United Nations Building.

The Secretary General was there to receive and took them to a room for briefing.

"I have called an emergency session, on my invitation just said 'Out of the World Gathering', how they interpreted, I left to their imagination. Some Presidents and Prime Ministers called to clarify, but said to them, it be an honour for your country to be present on this historical gathering.

I understand that you have a recorder to hook up, I will take you to our recording section and get it connected there. On a signal from you, they will play it."

"Excuse me Mr. Secretary General, the recorder I have cannot be hooked to anything you have. Steve may have told you, it was put by us into a Pyramid several millenniums ago, what we can do, I will place it in front of a microphone and play it. Kindly ask one of your men to put on the rostrum one with a short stand.

Steve, David, Jim, Sam and Daniel were seated in a room that overlooked into the Assembly Hall.

The Secretary General entered with Ayond, holding the device. There was an instant thunder of applause.

Ayond placed the device close to a microphone with flexible stand.

"Thank you, thank you," The Secretary General repeated and waited for members to settle down.

In the minds of all members was one question, "Who is that persons standing to him." Ayond stood relaxed with a smile.

Soon the Hall came to pin drop silence.

"Your Excellences, Ladies and gentlemen, it is a very special day in the history of this world body, and in fact, the whole world. That is why I have entitled this special session 'Out of this World Gathering'. It literally says what it means. We do have an out of this world, not a situation, but a person, yes, a person from another planet." He paused to let the low keyed commotion settle down. Noticed nearly all were turning their heads as where the person from another world is, "Will he be brought in in a cage?" Some may have thought.

"You don't have to look around, that person is standing next to me, be gracious to give a welcoming applause to Madame Ayond from the planet Urna."

There was a slight uproar of disbelief, but quieten down as the Secretary General began to clap requesting Ayond to the microphone.

The din seized.

The assembly rose and applauded suspiciously.

"Thank you," she said.

Ayond spoke, "Good morning your excellences, ladies and gentlemen, your first reaction when the Secretary General mentioned me to be an alien from another world, an element of doubt came to your minds. When a person of his calibre and status says something should not be taken with any shred of doubt. I shall extend an apology to him on your behalf. Yes, I do come from another world, and there many others like me."

There was a stir, shuffling and murmuring among the audience. Then with a loud voice she began, "Yes, extra-terrestrials from another world; what did you expect, a reptilian, an amphibian like your Hollywood depictions. We have evolved just like you into a beautiful race," she paused, "please bear with me and hear our story, after I finish my presentation, we can meet and talk.

"We came to your planet by accident and liked it. Wherever we went the people were hospitable. About fifteen thousand years ago, our spaceships landed, of course I was not there at that time, and I was born here on Earth. My ancestors first landed in the land of five rivers which you call today, Pakistan. After some years, moved to the land of two rivers, the Euphrates and Tigress, then to the land of the Nile. Explored all the continents and islands, built many monuments, mainly as land marks and to please the people living there. Just to name one, the Sphinx with the head of then chief of the tribe whose hobby was to hunt lions, people loved it, and at one stage began to worship it.

"In the early days we surveyed the planets flora and fauna starting from the north of Great Britten, the continent of Europe, Asia, Australia, the Americas and Africa. We familiarized ourselves with the habits and beliefs of the people and respected them. We found your world to be unique in many ways, it is beautiful and decided to make it our home, and be your guest.

"However, at that time, a message was put in one of the Pyramid to be retrieved by future generations to tell them who we were, and what contributions made by us. But we are lucky to be still here on Earth.

"From Egypt we moved our headquarters to Great Britten, because of serious weather conditions, there were floods and a series of earthquakes, for a time we thought the Nile would change its course to empty in the Red Sea."

There was a brief and loud laughter, Ayond was not pleased and with a face of annoyance, she continued, "I get the hint, some of you are getting bored, however, let me continue, a message was left therein, of what we thought of the human race and what it would be like in the future. We have translated the text as it was in our language, and will read it out to you through the very machine it was recorded within. Please be attentive."

The baritone like voice began, "People of this world, I greet you, when we first came to your world it was in a state when you were innocent people lived day by day with no interests accept, eating, looking after children, make war and kill animals for sport.

"What great strides in development you must have reached if you are listening to me, is commendable. It means you have reached a stage of high technological achievement. Our contribution to teach you agriculture, basic sciences and the like must have been a great help to catapult you in a realm of peace, harmony, free from disease, poverty and wars.

"I am confident you must have outlawed all form of anger and live like a family, busy in search of knowledge to reach the zenith of perfection, and distribute your fruits wisely to others.

"There are many worlds like yours, some in the stage you were in, some lived in caves, some very highly advanced and some perished due to natural causes or wars. The vastness of space is so great, cannot be measure. The mechanism by which it was created took a very long time to evolve from one stage to another until it was ready to bring out life, through elements embedded *within the matter that created this Universe*. I do hope you understand the value of being alive?

"The Planet we came from is called Urna, very old, one and half times as old as the Earth, it had two suns, suddenly it began to have a gravitational anomaly effecting our world, its orbit and rotation. It began to wobble and fall free in space, we were doomed.

"Many years before this happened while exploring the Universe, we were lucky to have found on a lonely world a highly sophisticated machine that can command anything, *and it is done*. With its wisdom it manipulated our Planet's gravitational field and its course in space, like controlling a spaceship. That machine has been called by its builders as was written on it, the Super Machine and we renamed it, the Supreme High. It was this machine that has put this message for you. He is eternal as far as we know.

"It has taught us to behave and respect each other and had given us wisdom and rules to abide by. We respect and hold him in high regards as an Entity not a machine.

"When we settled next this mighty river and built many monuments and the body of a great beast with the head of the ruler of the land. He was a brave person who kills beasts for sport single handed, he was dark coloured and handsome, had many women. The artefact we built in his honour was for his friendship, and also to serve us as a guide to spot our location while flying in our vehicles.

"With your wisdom you will understand what I mean. We showed you the path by which you can achieve eternal happiness, and not to fall for misguided misrepresentations by the ignorant and weak minded, who for their own selfish ends want to usurp what you have. They were times when people thought we were some supernatural spirits, seeing our flying ships, they called us gods. We did not approve, but they continued, decided not interfere, wisdom in the future will tell them otherwise.

"All things have a beginning and an end; plants, suns and galaxies, but in between make the best if it, enjoy the beauty of living, and contribute more to it for yourselves and others. The acts of anger in any form will only bring destruction, and you do not want to perish for its sake.

"A final note of advice, before I end, be good and wise, for there are others in the stars watching you. They don't like dangerous neighbours. It is a beautiful planet you live in, enjoy it."

With that he ended and Ayond took the floor. "That was the message of long ago but now I have another message from our Head on Earth, the Supreme High who has kindly made a few suggestions that might be useful to mankind.

"Before I put it on, what do you think of the speech you just heard? Any questions?"

There were several hands. "Any one," She said pointing aimlessly.

Someone got up, "How do we know this is genuine. Not an American trick?"

"No tricks, you are free to accept it or not. Soon you will know the truth, then it will be too late." Yes you, pointing at someone else.

Another member asked not getting up, "Do you want us to believe that we did not build the Sphinx and Pyramids? And that tape recorder of yours is thousands of years old. We are not children to believe fairy tales. How does the UN entertain such rubbish?"

"I have nothing to say, anyone else?" She was brief and curt.

"I am from India, can you help us to get rid of the trouble we are in. I mean the virus."

Ayond was glad that someone has brought up the subject.

215

"Please to tell you sir, we are working on it. Hopefully soon we will get rid of it."

"Excuse me Madame," a voice from nowhere addressed her. "Where are you hiding your people for so long? Why did you not come in the open before, why now?"

"Because it would have caused social upheaval, many of you would have created trouble for us. Now is different, you are at war somewhere, and your planet is plagued with a deadly virus about to destroy all life and before it does we thought of telling you of our presence, only we can help you."

"No thank you, we can help ourselves." Was his rude remark.

"Yes, you are helping yourselves by destroying your world, what have you done to get rid of the virus?"

Several questions were asked in the negative, some used unacceptable words almost insulting, while others suggested the United Nations should be shut down as it served no purpose, and has become an instrument of the West to propagate fear and threats to the innocent people of the developing world.

The commotion became unpleasant and some members began to walk out. More commotion and noise triggered Ayond patience.

She realized that in this body of elite representatives of world governments, it would be of no use to continue any further. They would react to the Supreme High's message the same way. Not to read it out. She began to collect her equipment and excused herself to leave when the Secretary General held her by the hand and, "Please wait, I want to say something before you leave."

He stood for a while staring blank at his audience. His facial expression was that of anger, he thought for a while, to tell them of what he thought of them, "I am sorry to realise that our world has not yet learnt to be courteous to guests especially those who come from far away sister planet, an advanced civilisation many folds more knowledgeable than we are, your attitude make you an ignorant and uncivilised bunch of hooligans," he knew that he being uncivil and continued, "The message in that machine took it for granted that by now we have become civilized and conquered the old ways of ignorance, unfortunately it is not to be so, you will learn the hard way. I am going to request Madam Ayond not to do anything to the virus, you should get rid it or 'it' should get rid of you.

"You tell your governments what I said verbatim. On behalf of this World Body I apologise to our noble guest for the reception she got from some members. The silence of other members, the so called Super Powers perhaps felt the same as you all did, otherwise someone should have spoken to the contrary. With deep regret I want to put in my resignation as Secretary General of this uncivilized body of unruly ..." He stopped from completing his sentence.

The Super Powers felt that had they openly accepted the voice of the machine, there would have been more repercussions.

The commotion was unbearable, everyone was talking, some loudly making abusive remarks and gestures. "That is us humans, we are doomed," the Secretary General remarked.

Suddenly there was a loud voice coming from the audience. It kept repeating the words through the microphone, banging at it to be heard.

The Secretary General moved his head in all directions trying to see who was making that racket. He spotted not too far from him was a delegate who had his hand up waving a handkerchief, reciprocating he waved back and spoke loudly on the microphone, "Yes sir, I can hear you, what can I do for you."

It was the Bangladesh ambassador, "A few of my colleges want to stay and hear the rest of the message."

The Secretary General turned to Ayond, before he could say anything she responded. "Yes of course, it will be a pleasure. But I suggest that we wait a while for those who have decided to leave, we can have a peaceful sitting free from any interruptions."

Most of the delegates left leaving a few that dotted the assembly hall including the ambassadors of the Western nations. When order was restored, Ayond spoke.

"Gentlemen, the message of long ago has concluded. But I have another message from our boss whom we call the Supreme High.

"As explained to you earlier, the Supreme High with his guidance we learnt many things, our survival depended on him when we were in danger of losing our planet, because of him we are in your world. However, his message is brief but worth listening to." She switched on the machine.

"Ladies and gentlemen, Ayond my ambassador to your highly esteemed organization has contributed tremendously to our stay on your world since taking over from her predecessor in your late 19th century, don't judge her age by your standard, she is just under fifty by ours, a budding flower if you may."

He paused for a while then continued, "Now I must thank all the people on your planet who has helped and made our stay most comfortable, mainly the British Government as we have our main facilities on their soil.

"We also have some small bases in other parts of the world, cannot mention them but only known to some of the people there.

"You have reached an impressive leap forward in technology, especially during the past two hundred and fifty years. You could have achieved much more earlier but certain elements have stood in your way. What I am noticing now is that you are facing another retarding factor, you are perhaps in the brink of economic and environmental collapse. I do not intend to elaborate on this, it is our policy not to involve in matters concerning your affairs.

"The moment we see that you are about to destroy your planet we will leave and find another home. Now to change the subject."

The voice paused for a long one minute. Silence filled the hall, all sat pinned to their chairs facing Ayond. Her thoughts were running wild as to what the Supreme High had said to leave this planet should it becomes necessary. Is he hinting at the uneasy situation in the Middle East, are they going to blow the world apart. What is he thinking?

The voice came back, "Most of you know about your solar system and beyond. The universe you live in, the galaxy you belong to and the countless other galaxies but what about other universes like the one we are living in. I will put it simple, your scientists are studying the possibility of other universes.

"They are on the right path, there are many other universes with different structure and different life forms. When one universe collides with another, they merge and in due course the structure of both will infuse, forming a novel forms of stars, planets, and ultimately life forms. Life will evolve to something far superior to what you can imagine. In brief, they would then enjoy the 'know how' of being alive.

"From our study, we suspect that your universe was formed as result of two universes colliding. You have inherited a brain so complex, you only use a small fraction of its capability, what if you are capable of using it in full. You will call yourselves gods.

"We travelled to many planets and met its inhabitants, but nothing like humans. You are unique. Your calendar speaks of two millenniums. Became intelligent homo-sapiens maximum about 40,000 plus years ago. You began to emerge as a social society, to build structures, pursue knowledge and build weapons hardly under 10,000 years, but only in the past few hundred years you began to leap forward in technologies that were taboo, and finally only in the last century the doors opened, and catapulted you into an information age."

The Secretary General looked at Ayond and shook his head in appreciation of what he has heard. Suddenly some members who had walked out came back and took their seats. Ayond switched off the equipment and waited for the arrivals to settle down. Perhaps after reporting to their governments the scenes that had taken place earlier, they were reprimanded and told to return. Moments later she switched it on. The voice continued.

"I hope I am not boring you, but bear with me just a few more minutes. Think seriously of what I have said, let it be your homework. I am sorry to see how some people hate each other, going to the extent of annihilating one another and in the process perhaps the whole of mankind.

"Some of you here who are not directly involved in what is happening in some part of the world, may report to their governments to be prepared for the worst and precautions should be made for the survivor of their people and work together with those likeminded to rebuild a new world of peace eradicating wars altogether.

"I leave you now, and please don't ruin this beautiful planet."

With those closing word Ayond looked at her audience, what she was staring at, were frozen faces perhaps still digesting the warning that might befall mankind.

Ayond thanked them and wish them good bye. She gathered her equipment and the Secretary General escorted her to where her colleagues sat and watched.

At the hotel Steve called for a meeting with all. He summed up, "It is of no use to try get them understand the situation. All are suspicious of each other. I suspect even the Super Powers are doubtful of your intensions. I think those who stayed behind will report the situation seriously to their governments, it may have an effect on other nations.

"Let's leave it at that, meanwhile, please do what you can to rid of the pest for humanity's sake.. Tomorrow night we leave for home, you are free to go sightseeing if you wish. I have some official business to conclude, we'll meet some time tomorrow around 4 in the afternoon and if you need me you have my phone number." Steve said.

# CHAPTER 32

**Back in London** Steve reported to the Prime Minister the failure of their mission to the United Nations. "Most of the nations did not believe in what was said, some branding it as an American conspiracy," He reported.

The Guardian was sorry to hear the report, "I pity the Americans, they do so much for those nations by giving them money allow them to visit their country, educate them and what not, in the end they are the bad guys. The British, Germans and French are in the same boat. The western foreign policy, if anything has failed.

"The war has pushed the warring factions back thirty years to recover, soon they will go begging and as always the West will oblige. Just because they have the resources and their enviable strategic locations. Once the Canadian oil reserves come to maturity, most of it is still untapped, and the advancement in the agricultural field of the great nations of the West; those nation will no longer have a clout. The world would be different, the psyche will change, perhaps trigger the beginning of a new world order."

He paused, and waited several minutes before he spoke.

"Let's concentrate on the virus issue. I have alerted our flying discs crew to check all vehicles even the mother ship and smaller transporters to be space worthy. We'll need just a few ships to do the snow job, and the others for a greater plan. I will disclose to you in the next couple of days after getting the Supreme High's final decision.

"Take David and the rest of the team into the vehicle that will create the clouds and the snow. This will give them first-hand knowledge how it feels to be in a flying saucer as humans call it," the Guardian concluded.

Ayond was getting more anxious to know what the Guardian is keeping from her. Why all the space ships are being serviced, and the mother ship, "Are we going somewhere, perhaps back to Urna?"

The team was more than exited to get a ride in a flying saucer. "We'll do it in the day time, let those non-believers see that we exist and do the good deed. Only then they will try to contact us but it will be too late. They have missed the golden opportunity to know us and benefit from our knowledge, they will regret it the rest of their lives."

The day arrived and the team along with Ayond and Aishtra boarded a bus and drove off to an isolated country side. Little hills doted the area, the bus stopped in front of a large warehouse. A door began to slide open. The bus drove in and parked a few feet from the entrance.

They got off and looked in amazement at the size of the structure. They could see nothing inside, then a few feet away from them another door began to slide open.

In front of them stood a circular vehicle on a tripod about fifty feet in diameter.

"So that is a flying saucer in person," Sam exclaimed.

"Unbelievable, what a piece of art," David murmured.

Four figures approached them from far. They wished Ayond first and the rest shaking their hands. Two men and two females.

"They are all from Ayond's planet," Aishtra whispered to Sam.

They followed them to the ship. They entered a circular elevator, it ascended slowly with all huddled close to each other. There was a click, and the door opened. They were in a circular room, glass widows all around, centre front a dash board indicating the operational instruments of the vehicle with two crew, sitting.

"Gentlemen, welcome aboard," one of the crew said and pointed to seats on their either sides. "Sit anywhere and enjoy the scenes on the outside." As they sat, chairs sucked each of them from below and back.

"With that suction you are secured well into your seats, better than belts," Ayond explained.

Minutes later, there was a soft hum of the engines, several lights blinked on the dash board, no sign of a steering wheel, the pilot and co-pilot played around with some buttons and the vehicle began to move forward.

After clearing the warehouse, it stopped for a while and the pilot's announcement came through a speaker. "We will fly at 70,000 feet, we'll start from Iran first, then sweep across to Iraq, Syria and its neighbours coming down to Saudi Arabia and Yemen. Before and during the formation of the clouds and snow we will fly low for the public down below to see us."

David looked at Ayond, "What about India, China and the rest."

"Other crafts were sent to different locations. We instructed them to make themselves seen to the people below before creating the clouds and snow as we will be doing."

Minutes later, there were on Iran, they flew low over the capital city and other town for the people to see their acrobatics and display their presence. After several manoeuvres, the craft ascended and returned to its eastern borders.

"Now to start our performance, there will be nothing visible at first, then gradually thick cumulus clouds will begin to form." They flew all over the entire country until their skies were completely covered by thick grey clouds. Returned back to where they started, and captain said, "We are now feeding the clouds with pallets, and shortly after snow will form and fall for many hours continuously. The whole country will be covered with at least three feet thick snow which will eventually turn to solid ice and will last for several days."

"People down below must have seen our performance, but have no idea why. It will dawn on them when the snow does its act by eradicating the bug, at least they would know that we the aliens have done it. It will be too late to thanks us, as we may not be there." Ayond said sullenly.

The craft moved from country to country allotted to them. In Saudi Arabia and Yemen who had never seen snow, ran mad to take shelters in their homes.

That night television broadcasts showed the unprecedented snow falls on deserts and tropical areas where the normal temperature exceeds 80 degrees F. "It was reported in some parts of the world flying saucers were seen, some said that it was them who created this phenomena. It further stated that the extra-terrestrials tried to warn the members of the United Nations of the virus epidemic and how they can help. Instead a member ridiculed and blatantly rejected the offer and said......;" Ayond switched off the television and shut her eyes.

A week later it was announced worldwide that the snow administered by the aliens has eradicated the virus which has taken the lives of about half of the world's population. The broadcasts also requested the aliens to contact the authorities who want to express their gratitude for their kind gesture.

The Guardian was sitting with Ayond when listening to the news. "Too late for that, what we have done was a humane gesture, we don't need their applauses or gratifications. Just wait a few months when they will revive back to their old habits and enkindle their aggressive scores," He said.

The next few days the team spent their time going through books and artefacts at the library cum museum.

Sitting in the garden sipping tea, talked about what would happen to them as the medallion affair has ended, "They would be sending us home," David said softly, then continued, "I am beginning to like it here, the world we live in is full of lies and hypocrisies. There are hundreds of religions and all believe in theirs blindly. Who is right? Why the creator is hiding away, why can't he make an appearance just once and meet his people and put some sense in them. He can give the final order, to live as He commanded it or else.

"There would be one religion, no conflicts of who is right, and live in harmony, spend time in fighting disease and poverty. Enjoy the beauty of the Earth. But come to think of it more positively, humans, would manipulate His new Commands and split into factions, repeat their modus operandi as they have done in the past."

"Imagine a world with one government, one social order, one economy and one religion," Daniel spoke philosophically and sipped his tea.

David looked at Daniel and in a sarcastic tone, "The world would be boring with no politicians, no mafia, no dictators and no oil crisis. Do you really believe in a new world order? I don't think will succeed, even if they tried."

"All said and done, I am interested in the here and now, how about calling Ayond and find out what is in store for us," Sam interjected.

"Tried several times, no response. Aishtra too, with the same results." David said.

Jim looked at him, "What is the urgency, what is going to happen will happen, sit and reflect."

# CHAPTER 33

**The next day** while the team was lazing in the garden, Ayond called.

She came alone.

She was not that cheerful person, her facial expression was that of someone to convey an unpleasant tidings.

"You don't look too happy, are you not well?" David asked showing concern.

"No, I am well but have some unpleasant news. Let's sit down, and listen to what I have to say.

"The Middle East war may have stopped exchanging bullets but the leaders are continuing their verbal diarrhoea of aggressive words against each other which will definitely intensify into war.

"This time it will escalate to a world war. We have inside information that the Super Powers are contemplating in aiding some factions on both sides of the fence, and we don't want to be around when that happens."

"What are you trying to tell us," David was concerned, "Are you thinking of leaving, to where?"

"Please do not interrupt me, let me finish. From our reports nearly three billion lives were lost because of the virus. There will be hunger, social upheaval and in some parts of the world cannibalism was reported.

"The Supreme High after analysing the situation decided that we must not get caught in their quarrels or miseries. He said, and I quote, 'We have done enough. The people here are not like some of the races we had encountered in the universe. There can be no people better than those who built me, reached a great heights in science and technology, their lives gradually extinguished not because of war but a natural catastrophe, worlds come and go with different causes of extinction, in the case of Earth, it is simple to predict, wars.'"

All were listening to Ayond attentively. Sitting solid on their chairs, thinking of their own predicament.

"As I was saying, this will surprise you. Remember what I had told you about our planet that by a miracle it was caught up by your sun gravitational pull and had placed it into your system. Its orbit around the sun takes about twelve years, it is sandwiched between Jupiter and Saturn, and it is now due close to Earth than any other time during its orbit, in about 97 days.

"I had told you the how survivors on Urna rejected our plea to be friends, and held a grudge against us for leaving their ancestors behind to meet their fate. Years later, we literally shook hands when the Supreme High ad Guardian made a surprise visit.

"Recently the Supreme High informed them about the situation on Earth and told them that he and the entire people connected with him would like to return. They gladly accepted.

"In a nut shell, it is decided to leave. We shall leave with all of our ships, carry our entire work force, documents and important artefacts and leave this facility to the care of Steve's department.

"Any questions?"

No one spoke at first, trying to digest what she had said.

Sam was not at ease, voice almost trembling, "What about us, after all these days we have changed our life style, we'll not fit in our world, we will be out castes, at least for some time."

Ayond gave a big smile, in a comforting gesture she said, "How can we forget you. You are one of us, remember your last meeting with the Supreme High, his confidential report to the Guardian was that you are extra ordinary and must be included in our system, with all what is happening he has not forgotten you to be given a choice to join us to our world if you wish.

"You have been, forgive the expression, restructured mentally and physically, again the Supreme High's idea. He had it in his mind about such a situation, for that reason you were made ready to travel in space and be adaptable to our planet's conditions. He had prepared you physically just in case you decide to come with us. He had it all planned. You will adjust very well in our environment."

Again the team remained silent, perhaps trying to make a vital decision.

In his mind Sam was willing, he thought of Aishtra. Jim thought of his wife and two sons. David welcomed the idea of going, with a bit of reservation.

Ayond read their minds, "You don't have to decide right now. Tomorrow we meet in the library and discuss a few outstanding issues. I must leave, I just came to prepare you to have sufficient time to make up your minds."

Four of them sat contemplating. Each one lost in his own thoughts. Jim stood up and walked about the room. "How can I leave my wife and children? I have to stay, will adjust in the long run. My shop will keep me busy. I might write a book about our adventure"

"The change will do me good. Wife passed away, both sons are married and happy," David was comfortable, turned to Sam and Daniel, How about you two?"

"Happy to go, have no commitments, though will miss Michael," Sam said.

Daniel was not listening to them, he was lost in his own thoughts. David snapped his fingers, "Daniel wake up. What do you say, go or not go?"

"Can't make up my mind. What about my church, my ancestors who built it, will curse me."

Sam put his arm around his shoulder, "Ancestors are dead and gone, and you can build church where we are going."

"Now don't put idea in his mind. Probably people out there have their way of worship, if any. Let us not impose on them anything. First let's go and see for ourselves what the setup is like," David put in.

"You may be right Sam. I may be able to establish something there, my ancestors will be happy and the Lord will be pleased with me." Daniel comforted himself.

They spent an hour together debating the issue about what life would be like there, shortly after, they dispersed to their rooms.

The next day Aishtra called and requested them to meet at the library.

They sat with gloomy faces, no one talking, thinking of their predicament.

Ayond and Aishtra walked in cheerfully, "I was shocked to receive a telephone call from Saeed this morning."

"How is he, is he planning to come," Jim asked.

"He is already here, he called from the airport and I sent a car to fetch him."

"Here, he will see everything, expose ourselves?" Jim looked worried.

"Nothing to worry, we have checked him out, he is reliable and a good person. I will offer him to come with us if he wants to."

"You are a kind hearted person," Jim was appreciative.

"Not about being a kind person, when we see good people, we take them, there are very few now a days. Anyhow give him a nice welcome when he comes.

"Meanwhile I have to clear a few issues before he comes. Firstly about the sketch of a child found in the church and Michael's place. It means the coming of a new age, a new world order by the help of people from outside your world, depicting the chariot. Those people will be from your solar system, who they are, we don't know, they are very friendly and show you new ways to understand life; but my guess is, perhaps us from Urna.

"Another interesting piece of information I thought might be an interest. About the spiritual visitation by entities, they were the Jinn, to help understand the good from evil.

"How did we come to know about all this? Though Aishtra, the Guardian had a meeting with their King, to inform him of the possibility of the evil and selfish reptilian aliens return back once we leave. In that event requested, to act as caretakers to protect the human race from any threats that might come them, who had previously invaded Earth prior to their coming 15,000 years ago and were banished. They are somewhere in the solar system and waiting for an opportunity to return.

"The King explained that they had tried in the past to help the humans to behave as wars and evil doings are not an answer. Using their physical traits met good men and women in spiritual forms to guide their fellow beings to be good, peoples began to misinterpret those messages and began to impose their versions on to others, the exercise failed. Humans remained a thorn to them. After some persuasion, the King agreed, to keep vigilant, but will not interfere with their squabbles.

"Jinn are everywhere, on the moon and elsewhere in the solar system. The King of the Jinn, indicated that there is another race in the solar system, but was not at liberty to disclose there where about, perhaps he is confused, the only other life in the solar system, as far as we know, are the people on Urna, let us wait and see.

"Before I finish, Steve was informed about our plans, lastly want to credit Aishtra's vital role with the Jinn," Ayond concluded and turned to Sam, "Someday she will tell you the whole storey."

Sam blushed and winked at Aishtra. He put a straight forward question, "Tell me Ayond that shop you had in London, why so, you didn't need it?"

"It was just a cover to be in a cosmopolitan city, to keep an up to date visual of what is going on and perhaps meet someone who had something that belonged to me; like you for instance.

There was a buzz on the intercom. "Yes, bring him in. Saeed has arrived."

He entered, stood for a moment in a daze at what he was seeing. He looked up and around him, and at the smiling faces looking at him.

"What is this place, like an underground city, is it a film studio, and who are you people? Saeed was amazed and confused.

"Please take a seat, Saeed, just relax, you are among friends," Ayond pointed to a chair.

"You know everyone here, and could not have come at a better time. Will explain to you in detail a bit later, let me finish talking to these gentlemen, you can sit and listen.

"Now where was I, tomorrow we start packing and transport everything of value to the warehouse, and on to the ships. They are of different sizes and configurations. Some of Steve's men will be assisting. That is all for today.

'Yes Saeed, what made you come to the U.K.?"

"On a vacation, had your card, decided to contact you,"

"What I am going to request you, is to be our guest for a day or two, then go and enjoy your vacation. We have a lot to talk about, what do you say?"

"Would love to."

"Then it is settled, do you have any questions?" Ayond asked.

"Nothing in particular, but tell me, you all do not like the tourists I met. Actually, I suspected that you were geologist in disguise as tourists, for that reason, I helped you to take that box, to be in better hands than rotting in our museum. Just tell me, who you people are?" Saeed was eager and fascinated.

"Saeed, you deserve to know. But first, go with these gentlemen and Aishtra, they will take you to your room, and will explain everything. I will meet you later on." Ayond said and left.

He was taken to a room next to Daniel. For minutes he looked and admired the furnishings, looked at the garden, tuned back and said, I can't believe what I am seeing. All this underground, the bright sun shine out there, what is this place," He was still in a daze.

"Please sit down Saeed, I am going a beer, how about you. David said and asked Sam to oblige.

"Yes please."

"While you enjoy your beer, sit and listen, do not interrupt me, you can ask all ask all the questions after I finish.

Sam served and sat with the rest, and waited for David.

He began, "Saeed, we are all friends here, and we got involved with the people who own this place, as you did to some extent. It all started when Sam and Daniel found........"

David ended with, the sequences that led them to Egypt and their departure.

Saeed listened patiently, devouring the last drop of his beer.

The rest waited for his reaction.

Finally he spoke, "If I had not seen this place and the story told by a respectable man like you, I would not have believed a word of it," He paused, looked at Sam, "Can I have another one, please."

Sam went to the bar and fetched more bottles and handed them across.

Saeed sat and thought for a while, stared at each one of them turning his head from right to left. "So you are all human, except Ayond and she are aliens, pointing to Aishtra.

"Ayond is an alien and there are many more like her here, but she is not; she is a Jinn," pointing to Aishtra.

"A what? A jinn, you mean Jinni, the bad sprit." In an undertone he quickly babbled, his lips vibrated as if saying a fast prayer in Arabic, then quickly added, "Only black magic can bring them, are there some magicians here, too."

"Relax Saeed, no, there are no magicians here, no black magic or any of the kind. This lady here, is as gentle as kitten."

To set him at ease, Aishtra who sat quietly listening, got up and moved towards Saeed. He stood up nervously, she came close, and kissed him on the cheek. "Relax Saeed, we are not as bad as you think," she whispered.

"Who would believe me, that a Jinn kissed me? I am now convinced that they are gentle people among you." Saeed was floored.

Jim brought about the subject of the virus. "Has the virus done much harm in Egypt?"

"Not too much, lucky, some flying saucers threw a lot of snow which killed them. We were told some extra-terrestrials have saved us and the whole world."

Sam added, "Those extra-terrestrials; you sat with one of them earlier today, and you are their guest."

"You mean Madame Ayond's people? I knew she is a good hearted person, the world should kiss her hands for such a noble cause. How lucky you are to be in such company."

The conversation lasted for some time and decided to leave.

Saeed made a request to share a room with Sam. "We will talk more, besides feel more comfortable with someone, afraid to be alone."

"Saeed, you are big boy, lived with mummies and dug tombs, how can you be afraid living with living people?"

"Just for today."

"No Saeed, we will meet soon for dinner after that, hit the bed." Sam added.

Saeed could not understand the last bit Sam said, "Why should I hit the bed, does it have any significance to sleep?"

"No Saeed, it is just an expression, 'to go to sleep.'"

# CHAPTER 34

**The met at the library** the next day.

Ayond was apologetic to Saeed, "You heard the whole storey, sorry we were not straight with you in Egypt, but our mission was such, we were obliged to act as we did, you understand.

"Can I ask you a personal question? In Cairo you told me that you were not married, are you still single. I am asking, because I have a proposal to offer you."

"No, I am not married and have no plans, my parent passed away, have no body in the world except my uncle."

"Good, Very soon we will be leaving your world to go to our own. These gentlemen will probably join us if they wish to. You can be one of them. If you do, will be treated like one of us, and might find you a bride."

Saeed could not believe his ears, he thought for a while. "Give me some time to think."

"You let me know by tomorrow."

Saeed instantly replied, "Not tomorrow, but by the end of this meeting."

239

"Very good, how about you all, have you made up your minds. How about you David?"

"I am in, just have to go home and settle a few things."

"And you Sam?"

"I am in."

She looked at Jim. He wasn't sure how to put it, "Ayond, I have a wife and two sons, can't leave them."

"We have a place for them, go home and discuss with your wife, she will be happier there than what you have here, and we'll look after the children. If you decide, close your affairs, but not a word to anyone.

"And you Daniel. There you can build a church, even if you have no customers."

"How can I have a church when there will be nobody to visit. And how your people will react."

"You don't worry about our people, will not bother you, and do as you please, even if you worship a stone."

Daniel thought for a full one minute, then with a confident gesture he replied. "Well in that case, I am in. and on second thought I don't need a church, it is a house of stones, and here on Earth all faiths have something in stone they worship. I have been thinking of that for some time. The church will be within me."

"So it is settled, and you Saeed,"

"I have decided, there is nothing for me in my country. People have changed. They kill you if your colour is not right. I will join you."

"I am sorry to hear what you said about your country, it was our home too, for many years. To be able to travel in our ship, you will have to undergo a few physical and mental adjustments. The others have already gone through it. We start tonight."

The others exchanged glances. The eating of the fruit will be his first.

The meeting adjourned and were back in their rooms. They had dinner together and watched Saeed devouring the fruit.

Jim left the next day. His wife was not impressed by what he told her.

"Some crazy drug addicts put it in your head. That is a joke travelling in a space ship and settle on Mars or some God forsaken world. You must have gone nuts, you were supposed to go and help a friend's son, who was in trouble, instead landed yourself with some opium addicts. Tell me another storey." Jim's wife brushed the whole idea aside.

He had to try again. "I will be honest with you, forget what I had said about France. Come with me where I have been, and show you something to convince you that I am telling you the truth about going to another world, where you don't have to work. Our sons and their families can come too."

"You mentioned, there I don't have to work. If I don't, who will? What about you, get free meals too. What kind of world are you talking about? I am sure you are still under the influence. Show me where you have been, but no dens or drugs."

Jim made a phone call to Ayond and explained the situation. A car was sent and Jim and his wife arrived at the Facility. Ayond and the rest of the team met them. Jim's wife was confused. "What is this place, an army barracks or what?"

More of the facility was shown to her, "This is where your husband had been all these weeks. He was doing a service for mankind and we want you both with your children to join us." Sam explained.

"I will be damned, he was telling the truth, but why leave home?"

"Because," David explained, "Sooner or later this world of ours will be facing a catastrophe, do it for the sake of your children."

"The wife thought for a while, are you serious about flying in a space ship."

"Yes mam, otherwise how do we get to the new world? We are all together. We'll have a happy and wonderful life. It will be better than what we have here."

'Well," she pondered and walked away from them, she turned and called Jim.

"Yes dear," he promptly replied.

"It looks all right to me, and that will be a big change. I hope our kids will like it."

"They will. I will talk to them, nobody else must know. It will jeopardize our trip." Jim said.

In the car, going back home, the wife asked as to what is to be done with the shop and house. Jim decided to give them to his brother.

A job well done he said to himself. His colleagues congratulated him on his success.

Their sons opted not to go, preferred to stay and take their chances with whatever comes. "Then we must the house to them," His wife suggested.

Back at the Facility, Jim's wife and Saeed went through the drill of eating the fruit and the physical therapy.

# CHAPTER 35

**In a surprise move,** the British government broadcasted a special bulletin, to the entire world.

A spokesman read the bulletin, "We were deeply saddened by the resignation of the Secretary General of the United Nations, and it was due to the unruly behaviour of some delegates. In good fate, the aliens who had lived on our planet for thousands of years, were proud to share an artefact that they had embedded in a Pyramid long time ago with a message to mankind of their stay should they not be here when found. But, they are still here and they retrieved it to tell us of their contributions and how they foresaw then, would be the quality and progress of the human race. Unfortunately, it was proved to the contrary.

"Today, perhaps all of our species would have been wiped out by the virus which had taken the lives of nearly half of the world's population. We are still alive, thanks to them.

"As a final note to the world, if you continue to do what you are doing, do so and prepare yourselves for the worst, they will not be there to help you, especially after the fiasco at the U.N., would be sorry if they decide to disassociate their contacts with us."

With that broadcast, the world listened with some concern.

The Super Powers took the stand to act as intermediary between the warring nations, and suggested some reforms to politically troubled areas, but all their efforts went in vein.

The Guardian sat with Ayond, "Tomorrow we start to load the Supreme High, we have to dismantle some of the rooms and passage ways to move him out, and dredge a hole at the main entrance, remove that little structure above, and rebuild it again as it was before.

The next day the tedious work began. Using hydraulics lifts and miniature sized fork lifts, carried the five feet high cube gently and moved at snail speed to prevent any vibration that may cause damage to the circuits within. The operation lasted for several hours, but finally done. The Supreme High was successfully transported and loaded on board the mothership.

Ayond, Aishtra and a team of workers combed the Facility to check if any items were left behind.

The day of departure had arrived. All the passengers including the team, Saeed and Jim's wife were ready to board.

There were three ships, the mothership was the size of two jumbo jets, and the other two slightly smaller.

The mother ship stood majestically alone in one hanger. On an adjoining hangers the other ships and smaller crafts waited for the signal to depart.

Underneath the mothership, Steve socialised with the Guardian, Ayond and her team from Earth, "In about twelve years when our planet comes close to Earth as it is now, we may pay you a visit,"

Ayond said. With those words, the final moment arrived to say their goodbyes. They hugged Steve and walked into an elevator.

Steve shouted, "Don't forget to write!"

From the top, through a widow, they looked down at Steve and made their final gestures. Steve walked to his car and drove several feet away and waited.

They sat in a lounge with chairs placed in a semi-circle with a large screen in front of them. Ayond took a seat next to David, Sam next to Aishtra and Jim with his wife.

"These seats are specially made for high speed space travel. You must have felt a suction as you sat down, you and the chair are glued together, to put it simply. After rising to 50,000 feet above the Earth, our speed would begin to gradually accelerate reaching 500,000 miles per hour. Urna, our planet is now about 805 million away, should reach our destination in sixty seven or seventy days max." Ayond explained.

The roof of the hanger began to slide open. There was a low whining sound hardly audible, the mothership began to rise gently, on the screen, they could see the ground receding with Steve next to his car waving, the sky began to get darker, the ground below became featureless, and the whining faded.

The scene on the screen changed, trailing behind were the other ships, then they were gone. Each chartered their own path.

"What is worrying me, is a brief sentence by the Supreme High just before we loaded him on the Hydraulic lift, he said something about to watch Earth at the time Urna comes in line with Earth you will hear bad tidings. What did he mean, the only thing I can think of is the escalation of the war, but to what extent." Ayond reflected.

They were only two days out, when she decided to call Steve.

"We are only two days out, I felt like calling you, my sixth sense tells me something bad is happening." Ayond called Steve.

"The next day after you left we had an intelligent report that one of the warring countries acquired a few new type of bombs that kills people, but no damage to buildings and other infrastructures, we know of one nation who tested such devised two years ago. The question is, how could they gets their hands on them. We were told by that nation such devises were experimental and under lock and key.

"You timed it well to leave, thanks to your Supreme High, he knew it all along what is going to happen. I wish he was here with us to help us find a solution." Steve concluded.

"You know I tried, but he refused, as it is our policy not to interfere with local affairs. When people become self-centred they must learn the hard way. Steve, so long as we can communicate, please keep in touch. We are still close to Earth, it takes a few minutes delay in communicating with us, at least for the next few days."

David spoke softly calming Ayond as her voice was trembling while talking on the phone, she turned to him and said with tears in her eyes, "It is finally happening, soon the spark will ignite and the whole world will explode. The cradle of civilisation is going to be their graveyard."

David just put his hands around her, and softly comforted with some kind and loving words.

The next day Steve reported nothing alarming but his call two days later was the news Ayond and the rest of them feared might come sooner or later, Steve was fumbling with words, tremor in his voice. "It has started, the world has gone mad. Only this morning some Super Powers have taken side, I have to go. Will talk tomorrow."

"Humans have done it, God help them," it was the first time that Ayond expressed her feeling with reverence.

Two days past, not a word from Steve. Television broadcasts were hazy at times, come and go. Just then Steve called, they all gathered around Ayond, "We are all at war, some crazy guys used the bomb, yes nuclear and there was a response. Soon we will annihilate ourselves. This may be my last message to you."

"Steve, can you hear me, my message will reach you in about thirty minutes."

An hour later, he came again. "Yes I will try my best but with the war on perhaps all communication systems will perhaps be destroyed, and our lives will go back to the Stone Age; hope not, pray for us." That was the last message received.

Days passed and no news, the Earth became silent, perhaps for a long time to come.

The mother ship went into orbit around Urna as scheduled. Communication with the planet was established and gave clearance to land away from the city. It was just before sunrise when they landed. All stood in a line facing the sun as it emerged. That was their first sunrise on their new home ground. The sun rose gently spreading its gilded rays on the mother ship and on to the new arrivals touching them in greetings and welcome.

The End

Special thanks to:

Paul Jensen and Rasheda Kabir,
I appreciate your proof reading help.

Books by the same author:

The Fatal Flaw (1987) Published by, Arthur H. Stockwell Ltd. Devon, U.K

Journey To Life (2015) Published by, Wesbrook Bay Books, Vancouver, Canada.